FLYING HIGH

The Sonrise Farm Series Book 3

Other books by this author
The Palomino
Stolen Gold

KATY PISTOLE

FLYING HIGH

THE SONRISE FARM SERIES

BOOK • THREE

Pacific Press® Publishing Association
Nampa, Idaho
Oshawa, Ontario, Canada
www.pacificpress.com

Designed by Dennis Ferree
Cover art by Douglas C. Klauba

Copyright © 2003 by
Pacific Press® Publishing Association
Printed in the United States of America
All Rights Reserved

Additional copies of this book are available by calling toll free
1-800-765-6955 or visiting http://www.adventistbookcenter.com

All Scripture references are from the NIV, the Holy Bible, New
International Version, copyright © 1973, 1978, 1984 by the
International Bible Society. Used by permission of Zondervan
Bible Publishers.

Library of Congress Cataloging-in-Publication Data

Pistole, Katy, 1963-
   Flying high/Katy Pistole.
      p. cm.—(The Sonrise farm series; #3)
   Summary: As Jenny learns a new way to communicate with
horses and trains with Sunny for the big jumping competition,
she struggles to forgive Daniel and his aunt and to accept that
God can change peoples hearts.
   ISBN 0-8163-1942-1
      [1. Palomino horse. 2. Horses—Training. 3. Forgiveness.
4. Horse farms. 5. Christian life. 6. Virginia.] I. Title.

PZ7.P64265 Fl 2003
—dc21   2002029788

02 03 04 05 06 • 5 4 3 2 1

Dedication

To my children Mianna and Charlie.
I adore you.

Acknowledgments

Thank you, Chuck.
Your kindness and faithfulness are unequalled.
Thank you, Kathy Huggins.
You are a true friend and sister.
Thank you, Jan Smith,
for your friendship, your love, and your help.
Thank You, Lord. Once again You show me that life in
You is an incredible adventure.

But those who hope in the LORD will renew their strength.
They will soar on wings like eagles;
They will run and not grow weary,
They will walk and not be faint.
Isaiah 40:31 (NIV)

Contents

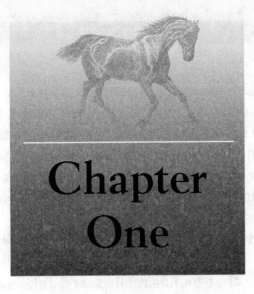

Chapter One

The rig creaked and swayed ominously as the terrified horses reared in the stock trailer. The policemen bellowed at the animals to stop, which made it worse. Jen bit her lip in panic. The whole thing, truck, trailer, and beloved Sunny . . . going over the cliff. Jenny heard the big truck tires start to slip toward the chasm. She grasped the chrome grill of the truck, sinking her heels into the ground, pulling with all her might. It was picking up speed. Now she couldn't get her fingers out. The rig was going over and pulling her with it. She screamed, threw her head back and screamed for Dad.

And there he was, gently gripping her shoulders, waking her. "It's OK, Jen. You're safe. It's over. We're at Mr. Wright's."

She stared wildly at the unfamiliar room, her mind swirling with confusion. Then her eyes focused. *Oh yeah, we arrived last night. I remember.* She threw her arms around Dad's waist and clung to him as if he were a life raft. He smoothed her hair and squeezed back.

"Daddy, it was terrible," she said with a hiccup, wiping tears with the back of her hand. "We were on the mountain and the horses were panicked and everyone was shouting at them. They were rearing and Mrs. DuBois's rig slipped over the side. I was with it, trying to stop it, and then I couldn't get my fingers out." She burst into sobs. "It seemed so real," she cried.

Dad held her, gently rocking her. After a few moments he took her chin and tilted her face back to look at him. "Sweetheart, that sounds really scary. Take a deep breath and look around you. You are safe, truly safe. Now take another deep breath and say with me, 'I am truly safe. If God is for me, who can stand against me?' "

"I am truly safe," she repeated. "If God is for me, who can stand against me?" Jenny felt the tension drain from her as though someone had pulled a plug. "If God is for me, who can stand against me?"

She leaned into Dad's chest listening to his steady heartbeat. *Lub-dub, lub-dub.* She sighed, rubbing her eyes. "What time is it?" she asked.

Dad checked his watch. "Five forty-eight."

"I may as well get up," she decided. "I want to check on the horses."

"Suit yourself," he shrugged. "You're going to have another long day."

"I know," Jen said, "but I don't think I can go back to sleep after that nightmare."

Dad gave a huge yawn, "Are you OK?" he asked.

She nodded.

"I'm going back to bed then," he said softly.

"See you later, Dad. And thanks."

He smiled sleepily, closing the door behind him.

She slipped from under the thick quilt and pulled on her navy sweats. She padded to the window. The sun was just peeking over the mountaintops; Sunny's pen with its seven-foot fence was barely visible through the trees. Jenny squinted, peering owlishly at first, then smashing her nose against the windowpane. *Where is she?* Leafy branches swayed in the wind hiding a section of the pen. The pen looked empty! *Impossible.*

Jen didn't believe her own eyes. She rushed down the stairs through the back door of the big house. *Now I'm scared*, she realized. The nightmare seemed like nothing. *Sunny is lost in a strange place.*

Dawn was here; the pink light bathed the barn illuminating everything. "Please be there, please be there," she repeated softly, over and over. She tried to keep it at a quick walk but by the time she approached that last corner of the barn, she couldn't stand it. She burst into a full run and flew around the corner.

Empty! The pen was really empty. The gate was closed. *Did she jump? Seven feet?*

The colt startled at Jen's sudden appearance and trotted around his pen, tail high, nostrils flared. *He is breathtaking,* she realized in spite of her panic. "Sorry boy," she whispered. "Did you see where your mama went?"

The colt was indeed staring at something. Jenny followed his gaze and spied Sunny grazing at the edge of the unfenced hay field. Behind Sunny stood thousands of acres of wilderness.

"Sunny," Jen called softly.

The mare popped her head up like a huge frightened deer. Jen could see her ears swiveling around. Sunny looked behind her as though ensuring an escape route.

"Oh no, sweet girl, you don't want to go there." *Please Lord, don't let her go into the woods.* Jenny looked past the mare at the expanse of property. Mr. Wright had told her last night about the wonderful unspoiled nature of this reserve. The North Mountains and freedom lay behind Sunny. *Will she trust me?*

She took a deep breath and started toward Sunny. She focused on her, watching carefully. The mare stood like a statue until Jen got half way across the field. Then she showed signs of bolting.

Jenny stopped. The mare slowly relaxed. As soon as Jen lifted her foot, Sunny lifted hers. *I am still too far away,* she realized desperately. *I can't even get close to her.* Jenny carefully placed her foot back where it had been. The mare did the same. Jen waited a moment and tried again. One step.

She waited, then did it again. One more step.

The mare snorted loudly swiveling her head toward the woods.

Jen waited.

Sunny seemed to relax once more.

Jen took another step. Sunny turned and careened into the woods. She was quickly enveloped by the trees. Her gold color made her invisible in the barely changing foliage.

Jen dropped to her knees, then sat. A single tear of helpless fear slithered down her cheek. She knew instinctively that the longer Sunny stayed out, the less likely it was that she would catch her.

"Lord, help me. Help me know what to do. You know Sunny better than I do. Help!"

A thought entered her mind, slowly, like a blossom flowering.

Jen rose and started toward the woods, about twenty feet to the right of where Sunny had disappeared.

Watch the ground.

It was as clear as a bell. He was telling her to watch the ground. She did.

Stop. Now take two steps to the right. She did.

Walk forward three steps, then stop. She did.

Jen focused on the clear commands she heard in her thoughts. She only got distracted once when she thought about how silly she must look. She couldn't even tell where she was anymore because she was concentrating on her feet.

Suddenly something grabbed her hair causing her to suck in a quick breath. "It's a branch. I'm in the woods," she said quietly. Her heart pounded from the fright of being poked.

Watch the ground.

Two steps forward. Now stop.

Jen was suddenly aware of warm sweet breath on the top of her head.

Sing.

"You are my sunshine, my only sunshine." Jen crooned very softly. "You make me happy when skies are gray." She reached out her hand.

Not yet, came the thought.

She drew her hand back slowly.

"You'll never know, dear, how much I love you. Please don't take my sunshine away."

Sunny's nose contacted Jen's hair. The mare whickered softly, snuffling and pushing Jenny's hair around with her lip. Jen heard an enormous sigh as the mare seemed to deflate.

Look up slowly, don't stare at her.

Jen looked first at Sunny's long, broken hooves, then knees, then her mighty chest. *She's put on weight!* Jen realized. *She's not thin.* Jen's mind flashed back to the last time she'd seen Sunny. In that awful woman's barn. *Vanessa DuBois. I hate her. She tried to kill Sunny.* Jen felt suddenly furious. In that moment Sunny stiffened and drew away. "Sorry girl, I'll think about something else." Jenny picked up the song. "You are my sunshine, my only sunshine."

The mare breathed evenly again. Jen continued up to her neck, then finally to her beloved face.

Now, reach out now. She did.

Sunny's body quivered as Jen reached up. The horse didn't move. Jen extended her hand, palm side down. The mare reached with her neck and contacted Jenny's hand. Jen's arm ached but she kept it out. She allowed Sunny to relax before touching her face. Jen rubbed Sunny's face while the mare pushed into her hand. She started at the nostrils and worked her way back until she finally made contact with Sunny's neck. She smoothed the mare's hair with her hand. The hair felt greasy from months of neglect. Streaks of dried sweat had crusted making salt ridges everywhere. Jen could feel the stuff collecting under her fingernails.

Sunny sighed again, relaxing visibly.

Jen inched forward and rested her head against Sunny's shoulder. She continued singing softly, her voice breaking. Tears poured down her cheeks, falling unnoticed onto the forest floor. "Sunny, I've missed you, and been so worried about you."

The mare continued snuffing Jen's hair and neck, almost like a mare with a newborn foal.

Another mighty sigh and Jen knew she could finally throw her arms around the great gold neck and hug . . . forever.

No rush, take your time.

Jen was suddenly aware of birds singing, and off in the distance, Dad shouting. She gasped. *They're looking for me!*

Her gasp caused Sunny to stiffen and snort.

Jenny forced herself to yawn, "No panic, no hurry, we'll stay here all day if we need to. We might need to because I don't even have anything to lead you back with. Will you walk with me?"

Jen began walking backward. Sunny followed.

Stop now. Turn around. She did.

Continue.

Stroke her, praise her.

Jen placed her right hand on Sunny's wither lightly and began walking. She kept her eyes trained on their destination. The mare followed willingly.

They walked that way, slowly, haltingly, through the trees, across the field, and into the barn. Jen led Sunny into a brood mare stall with a floor to ceiling sliding door. Sunny immediately made herself at home, pulling hay from the hayrack and munching. Jenny slid the door closed behind her. "You are my sunshine, my only sunshine," she murmured, half singing, half whispering. Jen kept her movements slow and gentle. Sunny blew loudly through her nose. "That's a good sign," Jen said with a smile. "I'm gonna' go find everyone else now. You stay here and eat the hay."

Sunny looked over her shoulder as Jen left, but kept munching.

Jen floated from the barn. *She's back, she knows me, we're going to be OK,* her heart sang jubilantly.

"Jenneeee," she heard Mom's voice calling.

Jen took off in the direction of the woods. She heard someone crashing around making all kinds of noise. *Is that just three people?* she wondered. *Thank goodness they waited until I caught her. They'd have scared her into the wilderness for sure.*

"Mom," she called, spying her mother's red shirt. "I'm here."

Mom whirled, "Jen, where were you? I was getting scared."

"You will not believe what happened this morning," Jen started.

"Jen, with you, I would believe anything." Mom smiled with relief. They called for the others and headed toward the house for a well-deserved pancake feast.

Chapter Two

"I've never seen anything like it!" Colton Wright exclaimed. "I can't believe she could jump out of that pen, it's seven feet high! It just . . ." His voice trailed off as he shook his head in amazement. "And I thought you said she was starved. She looks in perfect weight to me. Look at the head on her. Stunning! Jenny, they are two of the most incredible horses I've ever seen, and I've seen a lot!"

Jen grinned, nodding in agreement. "Thanks, Mr. Wright. I just adore her. She is more than a dream come true." Jen suddenly turned. "Daniel was there. He'll know why they look so good; he was feeding them."

"I don't know why she told me to start feeding them," Daniel shrugged. "Unless . . ."

"What?" Jen urged.

"Unless she knew she was going to kill them. She wouldn't want them looking bad when the bodies were recovered. That means she knew three months ago. That's when she suddenly changed her tune. It was right after she evicted Shannon Lockhart from the barn. I thought Aunt Vanessa had changed . . . but I guess I was wrong."

His voice trailed off sadly.

"I'm sorry," Jen whispered.

"It's not your fault," he snapped. "Quit apologizing!"

"I'm sorry," Jen said automatically, then clapped her hand over her mouth.

Daniel suddenly grinned. "You are sorry—the sorriest girl I ever met."

Jen grinned back. "You're pretty sorry yourself."

"OK, you two," Colton interrupted. "Enough. We need to start on the feeding. Hop to it."

🐎   🐎   🐎

After breakfast Colton started to explain his procedure to deal with the spooked animals. "We'll start with the colt. Does he have a name?"

Daniel nodded. "Fire and Fury. Aunt Vanessa called him Fury."

"Fury?" Colton repeated, looking doubtful.

"Don't let him fool you," Daniel warned. "They're both very dangerous."

Jen grabbed Daniel's shirt and dragged him into the barn where Sunny now stood chewing peacefully.

"How did she get in here?" Daniel gasped.

"She followed me."

"So you ran in the stall and trapped her?" he guessed.

Jen wrinkled her forehead in a frown as she stared at Daniel, "No, I didn't trap her. She followed me from the woods. She jumped out of the pen last night and I found her. Daniel, these horses aren't mean. They are terrified, which can *make* them dangerous, but they are just trying to survive."

"She's right," Colton echoed. "Horses are the ultimate flight animal. When you take away their ability to flee and *then* terrorize them, they can become very dangerous."

"So what are you saying?" asked Dan. "Can you fix these horses?"

Colton smiled sadly. "These horses aren't the problem. They are simply doing what they've been trained to do. We need to 'fix' the way they've been trained. You see, Daniel, every time you interact with a horse, you are training it. If you allow yourself to explode and get angry, you train your horse not to trust you. If you then beat or terrify the horse, you convince that animal that you are an enemy. These horses believe that we are going to destroy them. Their response to that is to flee, or in some cases to fight.

"We need to show these horses that we are trustworthy leaders. Jen has already done that with Sunny. Our challenge will be to convince Sunny that *you* are not an enemy, and to convince . . . what's the colt's name?"

"Fury."

"Fury, the same thing."

"How?" Daniel asked, obviously mystified.

"Walk with me," Colton said with a smile, "and I'll show you. Jen, would you like me to videotape this?"

"You bet!" she exclaimed.

"Stay here. I'll be back in five."

Chapter Three

The three of them approached the colt's pen. At the first sign of fear from Fury, Colton stopped them with his arms, like a crossing guard. "Jen and Daniel, let me do this first part alone. Would one of you get a bucket?"

"I'll get one," Daniel offered. "You want grain in it, right?"

"Nope," Colton replied, "just an empty bucket."

Jen and Daniel tiptoed off into the barn. Dan grabbed the first empty bucket he saw. "What's he need this for? The only way Fury is gonna' let us do anything is if he gets hungry enough. Then you offer him food and when he starts eating, *BAM,* you tranquilize him. I know this horse, Jen. It's the only way."

Jenny bit her lip.

Daniel handed Colton the bucket and returned to stand in the doorway of the barn. They had a good view of the pen, but were far enough away that the colt wasn't bothered by them. Jen glanced at Dan. He stood, squinting at the pen, arms folded, a harsh look of disdain on his face.

Please Lord, show Daniel that there is a better way, she prayed.

Colton strolled toward the pen carrying the bucket. He did not appear to be watching the colt. The colt was certainly watching him. At the first sign of discomfort from Fury, Colton placed the bucket on the ground, open side down, and sat on it. He turned his body so he was not facing the colt. He drew a small paperback from his back pocket and began reading.

Jen moved to the side of the barn and sat quietly. *This is going to take a while,* she realized.

After about ten minutes of snorting and trotting around the pen, Fury whirled and stopped on the opposite side of the pen from where Colton sat. He stared at the man looking alert but not terrified.

Colton waited another minute, then stood up slowly, stretched, yawned, and moved two feet closer. Fury took off around the pen once more. Colton pulled out his book again and began reading.

This time it took about eight minutes for the colt to settle down. He stood as far away from Colton as the pen would allow, his golden sides heaving in and out. He licked his lips and stared. Another minute later, Colton moved two feet closer again.

This is amazing, Jen thought. *He seems to know just the right time to move.*

She slipped a sideways glance at Daniel. He still looked unconvinced.

After what seemed like hours, Colton reached the pen. Fury pressed himself against the opposite side but did not seem panicked. Colton sat and read to himself. Fury looked lost. He licked his lips and tossed his head.

Finally after what seemed like all day, the golden colt

lowered his head and took a step in Colton's direction. Colton casually stood up and took a step away from the colt, but staying right next to the round pen. He placed his left arm on the bar and leaned against the pen. Jen heard him humming quietly.

Again, the colt moved toward the man. Colton took another step away. *They are playing Ring Around the Rosie,* Jen thought, grinning.

Fury took three steps toward Colton and then magically, began following him around the pen.

Colton stopped at the gate and waited.

Fury stopped.

Colton opened the gate.

Fury whirled and fled to the back of the round pen. Colton tucked himself inside, grabbing a long stick on the way in.

"See, Jen," Daniel whispered. "Colton is gonna let him have it now."

Jen waved her hand as though brushing away a mosquito.

The colt looked paralyzed by fear. Colton positioned himself near the center of the pen. Fury took off, pounding around the ring. Colton stood quietly.

For ten minutes it looked like Fury would continue forever. The pen was too small to really stretch out, but the colt tore around it like a wild thing. *I hope he doesn't go over it*, Jen thought anxiously.

At that moment Fury launched himself. He hit the top rail and fell backwards in a heap. Jen gasped. The colt scrambled back to his feet and took off again, his left foreleg bleeding profusely.

Daniel hunkered down next to her. She hardly noticed. "You OK?" he asked. She had to shake her head no. "I'm sorry, I knew it would be like this," he said, shaking his head sadly. "That colt is crazy. You'll never be able to do anything with him."

Jen felt white-hot lava rising up in her. "You did this to him," she hissed. "You and your stupid aunt."

Daniel stared at her, eyes sparkling with hurt. "That's it," he said, throwing up his hands. "I'm outta' here. Good luck, I hope this works out for you." He walked toward the house giving the round pen a wide berth.

Jen felt sick to her stomach as she listened to Daniel pull out in Vanessa Dubois's truck. She pressed her back against the barn and crossed her arms over her churning abdomen. *What are you doing, Colton?* She looked down for a moment. When she looked back up, the colt was standing while Colton used his long stick to rub him on the neck.

What happened, how did I miss that? she thought, staring wildly. Then it was a graceful dance as they moved back and forth. Colton used his stick only as an extension of his arm. He never hit the colt.

Fury responded by licking his lips and keeping his eyes on the man. His sides heaved from racing around, and he looked relieved to have found a friend.

Daniel is missing this! Jen realized. *I shouldn't have said what I said. Except that it's true. I am still so angry with them. Both of them. How could they do what they did?* Her heart took off down an ugly trail of blame. *Now I'm missing this,* she thought. *Vanessa DuBois is robbing me of my joy even now,* she thought bitterly.

Suddenly Colton was rubbing Fury's neck with his hands.

How did that happen? OK, I'm not thinking about anything except this. Goodbye Daniel and Mrs. DuBois, and good riddance.

She leaned forward, furrowing her brow. *Concentrate.*

Colton was clearly caught up in the moment. He began rubbing Fury all over. The colt stood quietly with a much softer look in his eye. Colton turned and gestured to Jen. She rose quickly and walked toward the pen. Fury looked like he was trying to hide his huge gold body behind Colton.

"Drop your gaze, Jen." Colton said softly. "Don't approach so directly, kind of mosey on over, like you don't really care where you wind up."

Jen stared at the ground and meandered toward the pen.

"Good, now sorta' walk around the pen like I did. Give his curiosity a chance to kick in."

The colt pivoted around Colton keeping his eye on this new human. Jen watched the ground and kept her movements slow.

"Horse trainers sometimes try to rush things," Colton said, loud enough for Jen to hear. "If they would just take the time the *horse* needs, they would get a better result."

"How long will it take?" queried Jen.

"It will take as long as it takes. He's not wearing a watch and neither should we."

Jen nodded. *That makes sense.*

"Jen, what you need to realize is that horses and humans are natural enemies. We are predators and horses are prey animals. That means they have survived by staying far away from guys like us. What we want to do with Fury is convince him that we understand how he thinks, what he wants, how he ticks. We can do that by approaching him on his level. We want him to want to be with us. Like Sunny wants to be with you. When you look directly into a horse's eyes, he feels threatened. Have you ever been stalked by a wild animal?"

Jen shook her head. *No.*

"I was in Southern Africa on safari and I came upon a pride of lions. One of the biggest lionesses charged my truck. She was not looking at the engine of the truck. She was staring at me, my eyes. She knew exactly what she wanted to rip open and it wasn't the vehicle. Scared me cold. That experience helped me to understand what a horse might be feeling when I stare at him. It's hard to feel comfortable with someone when you feel like you might be lunch."

Fury snorted out, dropping his head and licking his lips.

"He's thinking about it," Colton said as he smiled.

Jen continued walking around the pen.

"All right, have a seat and let's see what happens," Colton suggested.

Jen sat cross-legged on the ground.

"I'm going to show you several things you can do with your horses to show them that you think like a horse." Colton went through more exercises with Fury. The colt was clearly enjoying himself.

I have goosebumps Jen realized rubbing her arms.

"OK, let's stop for lunch," Colton announced without warning. "Jen, let's get some hay and water set up for this colt. Where's Daniel?"

"He left," Jen said quickly.

"Why?"

"Because I said something, something true, and he couldn't handle it. He helped make Fury this way." *Yeah, that's it. I said something and hit a nerve. That's why he left.*

Colton gave a sad smile. "Come on Jen, let's have lunch. I'd like to tell you a story about an angry young man."

Chapter Four

Jen's ears burned. "You mean you used to abuse horses when you trained them?"

"Well, I didn't think so at the time," Colton explained. "I used to believe that you needed to 'show the horse who's boss.' We did that in a variety of ways, and if you'd asked me then if I liked horses, I'd have said Yes. The problem came when I realized that the methods I used didn't really work. They solved the problem for the moment. The horse might get on the trailer after you beat him senseless or had ten friends drag him on and slam the door. But the next time I had to load that horse, he'd be even worse. I began to feel like a failure and a liar. I was supposed to be this great horse trainer and I didn't even like being with horses, and they sure didn't like being with me."

"So what happened?"

"Well, one day I was working with a colt, a colt younger than Fury. I lost my temper and started hitting. He *would not* stand still and I got really frustrated. I raised my whip and glared at this colt's eye. Do you know what I saw?

Jen shook her head.

"I saw the same terrified look I saw in Africa in my rear view mirror. I saw the same fear in that horse that I had had of that lioness. It made me sick. I realized that I was acting like a predator and the horse was convinced I was going to kill him. I quit on the spot."

"Then what?"

"Then my life fell apart."

"How? What happened?"

Colton shook his head. "I was angry, really angry. With everyone. I took it out on my wife. Began shouting a lot. The day I quit horse training I came in from the barn and started screaming. It's funny because I knew inside I wasn't really mad at Shirley, it just made me feel better to yell at someone. Well, she decided to go to her mom's house so she took the baby . . ."

"You have a baby?" Jen asked.

"Well, he's not a baby anymore," Colton said, smiling.

"Sorry," Jen said. "You were saying . . ."

"She never made it to her mom's. A drunk driver hit them and Shirley was killed. Little Patrick was badly hurt and almost didn't make it. He suffered massive internal injuries. His kidneys were . . . badly damaged. He's spent the last five years having dialysis twice a week. He needs a transplant. He's been on the donor list for six years."

"Where is he now?" Jenny asked. "Why haven't I seen him around here?"

"He's with his grandparents for a week. They live near the hospital."

"Wow," Jen breathed, staring at Colton. "I never thought someone like you could . . . or would . . ."

"What?" Colton smiled gently. "Be a jerk? Cause so much destruction? Let me tell ya'. I can't believe it either."

"Sorry," Jen murmured. She stared at the table wishing something else would come from her mouth. Just then, Dad burst through the door.

"Hi, you guys!" he panted. "What's for lunch? I'm starved. We hiked around the whole place."

Colton patted him on the back. "Chili, in the pot. Sour cream and cheese on the side, tortillas in the stove," he recited. "I'm famous in this neck of the woods for my five-alarm chili. Be forewarned, it's hot."

"Great!" Dad licked his lips and picked up a bowl.

Mom and Kathy filed in pink and sweaty. "Ugh, how can you eat chili when you're hot?" Jen's mom asked.

"Easy," Dad said with a grin. "You put the spoon in like this, then put it in your mouth, like this."

"Anyone said grace?" Mom asked, ignoring Dad.

"Oops, sorry," Dad mumbled. "Better late than never."

Jen ate her chili slowly, her mind tumbling over itself as she thought about the incredible story of Colton Wright's life. *What does that mean about Daniel?* She wondered. *Is there hope for him? If Colton could change from that to this, then so could he.*

"You need to forgive Daniel," Colton said softly.

"What?" She looked up startled.

"Where *is* Daniel?" Kathy asked, glancing around. "Daniel's always around when there's food."

"I said something to him," Jen mumbled. "Something sorta' mean but true."

"Oh," Kathy said sadly.

Jen took a deep breath. "He said he was outta' here. I guess he's leaving."

"But where?" Mom asked. "Does he have anywhere to go? What did you say to him, Jen?"

"He told me Colton wasn't going to get anywhere with Fury because the horses are so dangerous. I told him he and his aunt had made them that way and it was partly his fault."

Mom shook her head. "Why did you say that?"

"Because it's true, sort of, I mean I don't think Dan was *trying* to hurt the horses but he did and he let Mrs. DuBois hurt them."

"But Jen, he *gave* the horses to you. He could have kept them."

"Mom," Jen said with a snort, "he would have kept them if he thought they were worth anything. He gave them to me because he can't do anything with them."

"Jen! Those are ugly words. Daniel gave you those horses. You should be grateful to him."

Jen said nothing. Her heart pounded, sending wild emotions through her system. She stirred her chili, mixing sour cream and cheese through the sauce. The whole color and consistency changed.

"That's what anger does, Jen," Mom said almost in a whisper. "It changes your whole life. It muddles it and soon everything looks different. Don't let anger settle in your soul. It will rob you of your joy."

Too late, Jen thought miserably.

"What's eating you, Jen?" Kathy asked after lunch.

"Huh?" Jen jerked her head around, spilling the pitch-fork-full of shavings on the ground.

"I said . . . what's eating you?"

"Nothing," Jen replied, shrugging her shoulders.

"Come on, spill it."

Jen's shoulders sagged. "I don't know why, but I am still really mad at Daniel. I'm even madder at him than at Mrs. DuBois. I know he gave me Sunny and Fury, but I just keep asking myself, why? Why didn't he help me months ago? Why didn't he do something to help Sunny? Why did he wait until she was about to die? And you know what—he *still* thinks the horses are dangerous and *that's* why he gave them to me. Because he is afraid of them. It wasn't for any other reason. I'm glad he's gone!"

"Whew," Kathy said. "I'm glad you're not mad at me."

"What do you mean?" Jen huffed.

"I mean, you've decided a lot of things about Daniel without asking Daniel. Why don't you talk to him, ask him why he did what he did? My impression, Jen, is that he was really afraid of Mrs. DuBois. She had something on him and he was afraid."

"Doesn't matter. He still could've done something."

"OK," Kathy said with a shrug. "But Colton is right, Jen. You need to forgive Daniel and Mrs. DuBois."

Jen rolled her eyes. *Never.*

Chapter Five

"You are my sunshine, my only sunshine. You make me happy . . ." Jen hummed the rest of the song while brushing Sunny's sleek coat. "Sunny, you're the best," she whispered.

Sunny's ears flicked at the sound of Jen's voice.

"Let's go for a little ride. We'll go before anyone else wakes up." Jenny tacked the big mare up and headed toward the ring. She hopped up and took in a deep breath. *Thank You, Lord for giving me back my horse.* They walked around the ring on a loose rein for ten minutes before Jen noticed Colton standing by the gate.

"You look good together!" he exclaimed. "She looks relaxed and happy, Jen. Can I show you something?"

"Sure," she said, sliding down.

"I want to show you some ways to talk to your horse. Ways that make sense to the horse."

"OK," she agreed, intrigued.

"You and Sunny have an unusual horse/human relationship in that you have already established some trust in this horse. That's not something I see every day. I'd love to show you some ways to make that relationship deeper, if you're interested."

"I'm interested," she gushed.

"Well, it starts with establishing a dialogue. We want Sunny to know that we understand how she thinks and feels and plays. Now playing is not something this horse has done a lot of because of her circumstances so she should really enjoy this. I'm going to show you several ways to talk to her. First is with my long stick and line. It looks like a whip but I'm going to use it like another horse's tail. I'll use rhythm and motion to get her used to the stick. Then I'll gently swing it over and around her until she gets used to it."

Sunny snorted and stiffened as Colton brought the long stick toward her. He began lifting and dropping it on the ground near her approaching so slowly that she did not seem to notice. Before long he was gently draping it over her neck and hindquarters. Sunny dropped her head and looked sleepy.

"You try, Jen," he said, handing her the stick.

Before long Jen had the same result. A sleepy Sunny who looked ready for anything but play.

"Now let me show you something else."

Before long, Jen and Sunny were moving together, Sunny moving away from and toward Jen with light touches and signals.

"This mare is incredibly light!" Colton marveled.

"What does that mean?" Jen asked.

"It means she responds to a suggestion. As soon as she understands what you want, she does it. Have you ever ridden her without a bridle?"

"No," Jen gasped. "I have dropped my reins. Is that what you mean?"

Colton shook his head. "It's too early for that. Let's keep playing." They played until 10:00. Jen's stomach loudly reminded them that they had not eaten breakfast yet.

Colton glanced at his watch. "Oops, better quit for now. You take care of Sunny. I'll rustle up some grub."

"Mmmm, sounds yummy," Jen said with a grimace. "Sounds like worms."

She led the big mare into the stall and dumped sweet sticky feed into her empty bucket. The smell of warm molasses as Sunny crunched contendly made Jen's mouth water. Then she checked the water bucket before heading to the house for some "grub."

It was fascinating. *Why do the horses respond to this stuff the way they do?*

Fury looked as though he wanted to climb into Colton's lap. He did not leave the man's side. Jen had a memory of crossing the street holding Dad's hand. "You stick to me like glue," he would say. Well, Fury was sticking like glue to Colton.

"How does this work?" Jen asked. "It's amazing."

"Well, Jen, do you want the long version or the short?"

"Give me the long one."

"Weell," he began. "Right after Shirley died I did some soul searching. I had time on my hands. Little Patrick was in the hospital. Shirley's parents were really mad at me and told me to stay away, so I did. I just took off in my truck, never to return. I had a really bad blow-out on the highway. Almost rolled the truck. This old geezer pulled over to help me and we started talking. Turns out he was a horse trainer. We started talking horses and I quickly realized he and I were not speaking the same language. I was intrigued. He invited me to stay with him, and I did. For two years. He became my mentor and best friend."

"What about Patrick?"

"Patrick was better off with his grandparents. God was dealing with me. He used those years to show me incredible things. I used to break horses by tying them and dominating them. Each horse eventually came to a place where he needed to decide something. Would he decide to allow his spirit to die so his body could live? When a horse made that decision, to let his spirit die, he was broken and I could do whatever I wanted with him. That worked for a while. My mentor, Todd Huntly, taught me to get inside a horse's head, find out how he ticks, get a feel for why he does what he does."

"Well, you wouldn't have broken Sunny," Jenny stated flatly. "That's exactly what Daniel and Mrs. DuBois tried."

"You know what's funny?" Colton said with a chuckle.

"What?"

"People need the same things horses do and these methods work on folks too."

Jen stared at him. *What does that mean?*

"Really," he continued. "Our motivation is different, but people need love, communication, and direction. Horses are motivated by comfort; people are motivated by peace. The ability to sleep well at night, without fear or bad dreams." His faded blue eyes pierced her soul.

She stared at his face. *How did he know?*

"Have you been talking to my parents?" she asked, suspiciously.

He shook his head. "Nope, I've just been where you are now. Hanging on to something that's better off forgiven.

When you allow bitterness into your soul, Jen, you give evil an opportunity to whisper to your heart. You truly have a choice: listen to the Lord or listen to the Jerk, the ultimate Jerk."

"I'm not listening to the Jerk," she declared angrily. "I don't know what you're talking about!" She turned on her heel and headed back to the barn leading Sunny.

Who does he think he is? I listen to the Lord. I pray, I forgive. Good grief. Daniel is the jerk around here. He's the one who caused all this. He's the coward who wouldn't help 'til it was almost too late. I'm the one who discovered what was happening!

She began untacking Sunny, muttering under her breath.

"What's up with you?" Kathy asked.

Jenny jumped. "Oh! You scared me."

"Sorry, just came in from an amazing trail ride. Jen, your dad actually trotted. Hellooo, did you hear me? Your dad, you know, big tall blond guy, he trotted . . . on a horse . . . on the trail."

"That's nice," Jen mumbled, slipping the reins off over Sunny's head.

"Jen, you and I are friends, right?"

Jen glanced at Kathy. "Right."

"So what's going on with you? You seem angry and distracted."

That's it! Jen shouted to herself. "I am *not* angry or distracted and I sure wish everyone would just leave me alone!" She stormed out of the barn and headed for the house. *Lord. I am not angry, am I?*

No answer.

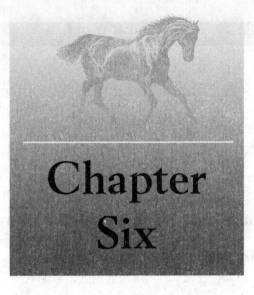

Chapter Six

The phone rang right in Jen's ear. She dropped the honey container with a clatter. Colton grabbed the phone and answered sounding annoyed. Jen's watch read 7:15. *Awfully early* she mused. *Wonder who it is?*

"Oh," Colton said. His face went white. "I see. I'll be there as soon as I can."

"Who was that?" Kathy chirped, slamming the door from her walk outside.

"That was the hospital," Colton said tonelessly. "Patrick has taken a turn for the worse. If we don't get him a kidney soon, we'll lose him. I've got to go. Sorry, Jen. I know we were gonna' play with Sunny. It'll have to wait."

"That's OK," she said sincerely.

"What's OK?" Dad asked with a yawn from the bottom of the stairs.

"I've got to go to the hospital, Patrick is very sick. His kidneys are . . ."

Dad didn't hesitate. "I'll go with you."

"No, you don't need to," Colton protested weakly.

"We'll all go. You need friends around you."

Colton looked around the room, then shrugged. "Let's go."

The hospital smelled like . . . sickness, injury, death. *Now here's where I want to spend my vacation,* Jen thought bitterly.

Nurse Linda escorted them to the family waiting room, pointing out the snacks and TV clicker. "The doctor will be in shortly, Mr. Wright," she said kindly. "Then you can go see Patrick."

"Thanks," he said, his voice cracking slightly.

Before long, Dr. Fitzgerald marched in. He shook Colton's hand and smiled, though his brown eyes were grim. "Colton. How are you?"

"Tell me about Patrick."

"Well, he's contracted an upper respiratory virus," the doctor explained. "In his weakened state, it's become very dangerous. It could easily turn into pneumonia. You'll need to wear a mask when you see him, for *his* protection."

Colton nodded and the two men slipped out.

"Let's pray," Dad suggested. They held hands, bowing their heads.

Jen's heart skipped a beat. *Is Patrick going to die?* Jen wondered, feeling a flush of shame. *Lord, I'm sorry about complaining about the hospital. Just let Patrick live!*

Just then Jen heard Colton's name come from the TV. They all jerked to attention and listened, still holding hands.

"And in local news," the attractive brunette news reporter began, "horse trainer Colton Wright has been hospitalized with pneumonia. No word yet on his prognosis."

"What?" Kathy was annoyed. Dad grabbed the clicker and turned it off.

Mom shook her head and continued praying. "Lord, *You* know who really has pneumonia. Heal Patrick and renew his kidneys."

"Amen," echoed Kathy and Dad.

"Hey," Dad muttered, with an intense look in his eye. "I don't think you have to be *dead* to donate a kidney. I . . . " He took off down the hall toward the nurses' station.

Jen glanced at Mom who looked shocked for a moment, then wordlessly stood up and followed Dad. Kathy stared at Jen. "Let's go."

"Go where?" Jen asked.

"Go find out if we can donate a kidney."

"Ummmm, won't three kidneys be enough? Does he really need *my* kidney too? I'm you know, kind of using it myself at the moment." Inside she thought, *Hospital, surgery, not me.*

"Well, I'm going," Kathy said.

"OK," Jenny huffed. "I'll go. But just to keep you company. I'm not giving away *my* kidney."

Kathy grinned. "No one will *ask* you to donate. It needs to be something *you* want to do. It's pretty major surgery."

Jen shrugged but followed Kathy down the hall toward the station. "We would need to blood type you and see if you are a match," Nurse Linda explained.

"I'm just here for moral support," Jen announced.

"That's fine, Hon," replied Nurse Linda, rubbing Jen's back briefly.

It doesn't feel fine, Jen thought. *Why do I feel like a coward? I hate feeling this way. Daniel's a coward and that's why I . . .* She caught herself in mid-thought. *I don't hate Daniel. I'm just really mad at him.*

What is hate?

I don't really know, Lord, she had to finally admit. *Tell me.*

Hate is the poison that comes from unforgiveness and unmet expectation. Hate is choosing to <u>not</u> love your brother. Hate always destroys. Hate is our enemy, Jen. Why are you holding on to him?

Hate is a person?

Hate is the fruit of Satan. It is his signature.

I don't want to hold on to Satan. What do I do?

Forgive Daniel. And Mrs. DuBois.

Jenny sucked in audibly. "I can't!" she whispered desperately.

No, you can't, but I can, through you.

Lord, I do not understand.

You will.

"Thank you all," Colton said, shaking his head in disbelief. "I don't have words to tell you how much this means. That you all would want to donate one of your kidneys to my son . . . it's amazing."

"Now we just have to wait and see who has the matching blood type," Dad said.

Jen felt a noose of fear tighten around her neck. *If none of them match, I'll have to give Patrick one of my kidneys. Please Lord, let one of them match. I don't want surgery right now. I've just found Sunny and . . . please. Not me.*

The phone rang at breakfast again. "Yes," Colton answered, eyes shining with hope. "Oh, I see." Hope dimming. "Thank you, Linda. Yes, you'll see me in a bit."

Colton plopped down in his chair. "I'm sorry to report that none of you is a suitable donor for Patrick. Thank you for trying."

Jen crushed her eyelids together. "I haven't been tested yet, she murmured."

"Oh, Sweetheart," Dad whispered, taking her sweaty hand, "you can't donate your kidney. You have to be at least eighteen years old."

"Really," she breathed, almost ready to break into tears of relief.

Mom nodded agreement.

"Come on, girl," Colton said from the doorway. "Let's go play with that mare of yours."

Chapter Seven

It was amazing. It was like the big mare could read Jen's mind. All Jen had to do to get a response was to think about what she wanted to do. Like backing up on line. Jen just held the lead rope and prepared to give Sunny the back up cue, but the mare was already moving back.

"How does she know?" Jen asked Colton. "I don't even have a chance to tell her what I want."

"Well," Colton answered, "horses are one of the most perceptive creatures on earth. They are experts at reading body language. She now knows what you want before you ask her. *That* is now her cue. It is probably nothing more than a special look in your eyes or the way you twist your mouth. We don't want her anticipating your cue though, so let's disengage her hindquarters and ask her to wait for a cue. She is absolutely the most willing animal I've ever worked with. She clearly adores you, Jenny."

Jen felt an overwhelming rush of love. "It's mutual. I love her so much." Tears welled up, drowning any hope for words.

They played with Sunny until 2:00, then it was a quick lunch and Colton raced to the hospital to see Patrick.

Jen spent the afternoon brushing Fury and riding
Sunny. She recalled Colton's words. *The first three games
are the foundation. Your friendship game must be played a
lot, especially with Fury.*

"Brushing is friendship," she quipped. The big colt stood
quietly, almost dozing in the sun. Jen stayed at his shoulder and outside the pen. She only brushed one side. "I'll
come back and finish you later when you move." She smiled
and rubbed the colt's shiny neck. He didn't lean into her
the way Sunny did, but he didn't drift away either. He
seemed to enjoy the attention. *Amazing transformation,*
she realized. *Wonder what Daniel would think. Or Mrs.
DuBois. Ugh. I don't want to think about them right now.*

She wandered into the barn and grabbed Sunny's tack.
She heaved up the saddle, then placed it back down on the
rack. *I'll ride bareback today,* she decided.

"There," she announced, buckling up her helmet strap.
"I'm ready to ride."

She led the mare over to the fence and used the second
rail of the fence to scoot on to Sunny's back. The big horse
stood placidly while Jen struggled.

"Oof, not very graceful, am I girl? I need practice getting
up on really big horses!" Once up, she guided Sunny around
the ring at a walk. After two trips around, Jen realized that
all she had to do to turn was to look in the direction she
wanted to go. It was almost eerie at first. No rein was needed.
Just look at where you want to go. Incredible.

It worked at the trot. The canter. Even over ground
poles. Even over a tiny crossrail.

It was the most wonderful feeling of freedom and harmony. *My dream, my favorite dream. It's been a couple of*

years since I dreamed that. And here I am riding my *Palo-mino without using the reins!*

Jen threw her arms out and allowed the wind to wipe the tears from her eyes. Her heart felt light and squeezed at the same time. *Thank You, Lord, thank You, thank You.* Jen felt her heart beat in time with Sunny's rolling canter. It seemed like the most natural, beautiful rhythm in all the world.

Colton burst through the front door. "Jenny, Mike, Judy, Kathy! Come here," he bellowed. Jen heard him from upstairs. She dropped her book and came running.

"What?" Mom puffed, holding her hand over her heart. "What's wrong?"

"We've found a donor for Patrick!"

"You're kidding!" Dad shouted joyfully. "Who is it?"

"The hospital won't tell me. Confidentiality. It's most likely someone who died in an accident. We need to get back. I wanted you all with me. Dr. Fitzgerald says Patrick is strong enough and the sooner the better. They are prepping him now. Let's go!"

The drive seemed endless. Nurse Linda met them at the door. "Everything is ready, Mr. Wright. Put this mask on and you can walk with us to the operating room to wish him luck," and she whisked him away down the hall.

Colton came back ten minutes later, mask pulled down, paper slippers swishing as he walked. "It's incredible," he murmured, with a far away look. "I've been praying for this day for fifteen years, and it's here. God is so good." He sat down and burst into tears, his body heaving with emotion.

Mom and Dad stood next to the chair and laid hands on his back, praying silently.

Jen stared at Kathy uncomfortably. It felt strange to see Colton, strong, wise Mr. Colton Wright, sobbing like a child. Jen wanted to do *something,* but what?

"Let's pray, Jen," Kathy suggested. "We need to pray for the donor and his or her family also."

They sat there for two hours. No news.

They went to the cafeteria in shifts. Jen could only stomach a peanut butter and jelly sandwich. By 10:00 P.M., she curled up on the sofa and dozed fitfully.

At midnight Dr. Fitzgerald appeared looking disheveled but elated. "It was like that kidney was just waiting for Patrick," he crowed. "It was turning pink and working before we closed him up. You may see your son now, Mr. Wright. *He* is even turning a healthy pink!"

Colton whirled and shot a grateful glance at Dad. "Thank you all for staying with me and praying."

Dad nodded and waved him on with a joyful grin. "Go! Go see your son."

Colton made his way to the door and Jen heard his paper slippers swishing swiftly down the hall.

"Well," Dad said, still smiling, "let's give thanks." He opened his big arms like a hen calling her chicks. Jen nestled under one of them with Kathy scrunched in next to her.

"Lord, You are our mighty God. Thank You for providing this kidney for Patrick. We don't know where it came from Lord, but please comfort the family of the donor right now. Thank You, Lord, for bodies that are healthy and for the gift of life. Amen."

"Amen!" they chorused loudly.

Chapter Eight

Jen just had two days left at Colton Wright's ranch. *Where does time go?* she wondered. *Not that a week is long, but honestly, it seems like we have been here hours instead of days. There's still so much to do with Fury. He's just not ready to come home right now.*

Colton helped Jen with the brushes and tack for the colt. Fury now nickered whenever he saw Jen.

"It's not that I'm afraid of *him*," she explained to Colton. "I'm afraid of *messing* him up. He's coming along so nicely and he seems to like you."

"Are you asking me to keep Fury for a while?" Colton smiled. "I'd be honored. He's magnificent and definitely a reputation maker. You wouldn't consider selling him, would you?"

"No," she said, shocked and too loud. "I'm sorry, I mean, no, I couldn't."

"OK," he said with a shrug. "Just asking."

They played with the colt for several hours. Jen watched, amazed at the horse's response to Colton. The colt watched the man intently but without fear. The fear had vanished and was being replaced by a growing confidence. When they left the pen, the colt followed closely to the gate then stared longingly after them as they disappeared into the barn.

Playing with Sunny, now that was as natural as sunlight and rain. Jen forgot about everything, even Colton. She glanced up once, embarrassed, as she realized she had ignored him for at least an hour. "I'm sorry," she moaned. "I totally forgot you were there."

He grinned hugely, eyes crinkling at the corners. "That's all right. I wish you could see yourself with Sunny. You two are poetry in motion. It looks like you are reading each other's minds. Let's get you on her and see where we are."

Jen tossed the rope over Sunny's back and climbed up on the fence rail. At Jen's cue the mare sidled over to the fence, waiting for Jen to hop onto her bare back. Jen's legs barely came halfway down the mare's big body.

"Comfortable?" Colton called from across the ring.

"Yup," Jen replied grinning.

"How are you at the trot?"

She responded by asking Sunny for a trot. Jen relaxed her seat to ask for a slow trot, then tightened her seat to get a big, extended trot.

"*You* are like a tick!" Colton chortled. "I've never seen such natural balance in a rider. You could ride broncs! Not that I would recommend that, of course!"

Jen replied by squeezing slightly. Sunny exploded into a ground-eating canter. They thundered around the ring once before Jen relaxed her seat and exhaled, asking for a "whoa." She did not even touch her reins. Sunny almost slid to a stop.

Colton was speechless.

Jen rubbed Sunny's neck, giggling helplessly. "The look on your face . . ." she couldn't finish. She had to dismount before she fell off laughing.

Colton could only shake his head in amazement. "You are gifted," he finally said softly. "What would you like to work on, since clearly you are way ahead of where I thought you were?"

"I want to work on jumping without tack," Jen replied without hesitation.

"We can do that," Colton agreed. "Remember, Sunny's not fit yet. We need to build her up slowly or she'll wind up injured."

"Absolutely!" Jen agreed.

They started over ground poles and cavaletti. Lots of walking and stretching. Jen learned great flexibility exercises. Every hour on the horse improved her seat and focus.

"Hey, Jen," Colton shouted from across the ring. "Wanna' ride one of my horses? We can work on some of the things you want on a horse who's fit."

"Sure," she agreed, sliding off Sunny's back. The mare was only slightly damp from her light workout. Jen walked her around for several moments before putting her back in the stall. She checked the water bucket and topped it off. There was fragrant hay on the floor ready to be eaten.

"You are my sunshine, my only sunshine," Jen crooned as she worked around the mare. A huge sigh from the mare told Jen she was comfortable. Jen kissed the velvety nose and slid the stall door closed behind her.

Colton already had Jen's mount ready and waiting in the ring. He was a wild colored bay pinto named Polo.

"This horse was a rescue," explained Colton, rubbing Polo's ear. Polo leaned into Colton's hand, eyes closed. "The animal shelter called *me* because they couldn't catch him. The warden who dealt with large animals was sick so they had the dog and cat guy trying to handle him. They were feeding him buckets of grain, if you can imagine. It's a miracle he didn't colic or founder. When he arrived, you couldn't get near him and his ears . . . man alive, he'd kick you flat if you tried to touch his ears. He's been with me for seven years now. He's my best horse and loves to jump. You two should get along famously. Why don't you try him in the rope halter? I'll just attach the lead rope on both ends for reins."

Jen nodded, rubbing Polo's muscular neck. "Hi, boy."

They went around the ring at a walk. Then she asked for a trot. He wasn't as smooth as Sunny and she got bounced around a little. His canter felt like a rocking horse, though. Smooth, rolling, and very easy to sit.

Cavaletti, then tiny cross-rails. Pretty soon they were going over 3'6. It was like flying. The wind in her face, the thrill of take-off, that moment suspended in mid-air. *If this was Sunny, it'd be perfect.*

"All right, Missy," came the unwelcome words from the end of the arena. "That's enough for both of you. You are going to be stiff tomorrow. Let's quit on a great note. That last jump was excellent."

Jen slid off and rubbed Polo's face. "Let's go eat," she suggested to the pinto. "I'll walk you out, then I'll make you a scrumptious creation of hay and sweet-feed. Chef Jenny at your service."

Polo followed behind, clearly interested in the meal part of the invitation.

They wandered around the barn, over the little bridge, down the trail for a bit, then back. A large hawk shrilled high overhead. It was a wild, savage sound. It reminded Jen of Mrs. DuBois's voice. *No not her, I haven't thought of her for days. Lord, why are there people like Mrs. DuBois?*

I love her, Jenny.

No, Lord, she gasped. *How can You love her? She's evil. She tried to kill Sunny!*

I do not love what she does, but I do love her. And Daniel. They do not know Me. Someone needs to tell them about My love.

Oh, no. You've got the wrong girl. I never want to see either one of them ever again. I will try to forgive them, but I won't talk to them.

🐎 🐎 🐎

Jen shook her head almost as if she could shake the conversation off. Polo followed her eagerly into his stall. She slid a hand between his forelegs. "Yup, you're cool enough. Bon appetit!" The horse waited for the halter to come off, then dove for his bucket. "Goodness," Jen chuckled. "You act like you're starving."

"Some horses never forget being starved," said Colton sadly, from the doorway of the barn. "He's one."

Ask him about forgiveness.

Jen stared at the gray-haired man as though seeing him for the first time. "Colton," she started haltingly. "How did you forgive the man who hit your wife's car?"

52

He looked surprised for a moment. Then ran his hand through his hair twice.

"Hmm . . . I think the person I had the hardest time forgiving was myself. Forgiving the drunk driver . . . that was hard, impossible actually. I finally came to a place of surrender, a place of brokeness, a place where I recognized that I could do nothing without Jesus. It was the Lord who forgave that man through me. I had no ability in myself."

Jenny stood, shaking her head, not sure how to respond.

Colton smiled warmly. "We took a video of Fury on that first day. Let's watch that and I'll show you how God uses horses to show me the way to Himself. Maybe you'll see it too."

Chapter Nine

They gathered around the VCR and Jen popped in the tape of Colton with Fury on that first day. Mom hefted in a huge tub of popcorn. "This is probably dinner, folks, cause I'm not cooking."

Jen snuggled between Dad and Mom on the huge leather sofa. It wasn't cold but Mom covered their legs with a cotton blanket. "This is cozy," she murmured.

Kathy had the recliner and turned on the back massager. "Wake me when it's time for bed," she sighed, closing her eyes blissfully.

"Now remember," Colton warned. "This is unedited so it might get boring. But it's a great picture of God's enduring patience with us."

Jen had almost forgotten how wild Fury had been. He shot around and around the pen, searching frantically for escape.

"We start with an individual horse," Colton began. "The horse is chosen in a variety of ways, but they are always chosen. They do not wind up here by accident. The motivation for teaching is love.

"No person encounters God by accident. God is the Initiator, and His motivation is love. We want to communicate to the horse that we love him and that we are trustworthy.

"We have several problems already. The first problem is: Horses and humans are natural enemies. Horses are prey animals, which means, they provide meat for predators. Man is a predator. Now maybe *you* don't actually eat meat. Doesn't matter. God placed our eyes in the front of our round small heads. Just like a bear, or a lion. That marks us as predator. Prey animals have large eyes placed on the sides of long heads. This gives them the ability to see behind them. To keep them safe from predators.

"Our other problem is that horses don't speak human. They have a communication system vastly different from ours, and they have no interest in learning English.

"In a similar way, God and man are natural enemies. God is holy, and man is not.

Man knows he is not holy. This creates fear and communication breakdown between God and man. Man avoids God and tries to find life elsewhere. You can see Fury trying to avoid me and find life outside the round pen. He's looking at the other horses in the field. He's probably feeling really sorry for himself and wondering 'Why me?' Well, Fury, it's because we love you.

"God uses time the same way I use the pen. It contains us, keeps us in a small place. He uses circumstances the same way I use the rope. To put pressure on us, cause us to look around. He allows us to run around and hopefully recognize the futility of escape. If Fury escaped, he would die. He's a domestic horse, unsuited to life in the wild. He would starve. We, too, are doomed apart from God."

Tears leapt into Jen's eyes. *Like Sunny apart from me.*

"Now you see Fury gathering himself," Colton continued. "He's going to try and go over. But he can't."

Jen winced at the sight of Fury impacting the top rail of the metal panel.

"Now he's thinking. He has come to the end of his own resources and still hasn't solved his problem. You can see . . . right . . . NOW! He has decided something. His eyes have changed. *That* is the moment I look for. It tells me he's starting to think instead of react. Now we have a chance to start a conversation. I'll start speaking horse, the same way Jesus came to speak 'man' to us."

Jen glanced at Dad. He seemed spellbound. No one was eating popcorn.

"Now," Colton continued, "I'll extend my long-stick. The first place I'll contact is his nose, and I'll let him make the first move. He's reaching . . . and there. He's touched the long-stick. Now I'll rub his friendly place up there on his withers. I use the long-stick the way a mare uses her neck. It's not a whip. All the time, I'm looking someplace besides his eyes. I don't want to challenge him or frighten him. Remember, predators stare at the eyes."

Colton turned and winked at Jen. "Jen can tell you about a certain lioness I met . . . Now Fury has come to the end of his own resources, needs a leader, and sees nobody but me. I am looking and acting friendly, and he chooses me as his leader. Horses need a leader. If I continue to behave in a trustworthy, nonpredatory way, this horse will grow to love and respect me and we can build a relationship that completely goes against our original relationship. We need God. We will find something to fill that need. God thankfully showed me that I was filling that God-need with all kinds of other things, mostly my reputation. That is what motivated me before.

"God used difficult circumstances in my life to pressure me into discovering what life is really about. His motivation was love. His method was communication through His Son, the God-Man. I have come to a place where I trust Him so much, that anything He does to me, through me, with me, or about me is OK with me. It doesn't matter how it looks to anyone, including myself. I choose to believe that it is for my best. He alone knows what is best for me. That is brokeness, that is surrender, and it is the most free place I've ever known."

The tape showed Fury standing with Colton, being rubbed and loved. The horse calmly following the man.

Jen's heart pounded as she wiped away tears. *Lord, is that what You want from me? Surrender?*

Yes.

I surrender.

She slept peacefully with no dreams of horse rigs and cliffs and falling.

Chapter Ten

Jammies, toothbrush . . . what am I forgetting? Jen asked herself. She plopped down on the edge of the chenille bedspread. She couldn't shake the nagging sensation. It was like a secret buried deep in her mind, struggling to reach the surface. *I'm not forgetting Fury, I'm leaving him here on purpose. And it's just for a little while. I'm gonna' have my hands full getting Sunny ready for show season.*

Colton was driving them home because Daniel had taken the truck when he went . . . wherever he went. "Hmm," she mused. "I wonder what he's doing. Probably back to that aunt of his, or under a rock." Daniel's inability to see the wrong he did still made hot white lava start churning in her stomach. She spent a pleasant moment imagining terrible things happening to him, and Mrs. DuBois.

"Jen, are you ready? We need you to load Sunny," Mom called from the bottom of the stairs.

She glanced around the cozy room one last time. "Yeah, I'm coming. I know I'm forgetting something," she muttered as she walked downstairs.

"I'll send it or you can pick it up when you come back for Fury," Colton said with a warm smile. "I'm sure gonna' miss you guys. It's been a great week!"

Jenny's heart pounded violently. "I'm going to miss you too," she said, her mouth twisting as she tried in vain not to cry. "I've learned so much this week, about Sunny and myself, and . . . " She lost it as he reached out to hug her.

"It's OK to cry, Jen. It gets rid of nasty chemicals from our bodies. Crying is therapeutic. Plus, I'm driving you home. You're gonna' be stuck in my truck for five hours listening to me sing to the radio. That's probably why you're really crying."

She laughed in spite of her tears. " I really enjoyed meeting Patrick. When does he come home?"

Colton's face lit up. "Next week, hopefully. Doctor says there is no sign of rejection. It's a miracle, really, Jen. It's like that kidney was made for Patrick. And the doc agrees that Patrick looks better every day. You could pray for continued healing."

"Absolutely!" she declared, meaning it.

"Well, let's get that big mare of yours loaded and hit the road."

Jen played with Sunny to warm her up and prepare her for loading on the trailer.

Fury cantered around his pen, tail up, whinnying hysterically, like he knew Sunny was leaving.

Jen glanced at Colton. "What's the matter with him?"

Colton smiled, "He knows what's happening. Horses are the most perceptive animals in the world, Jen. He certainly knows something big is happening. Why don't you let me load Sunny and you go stand over there next to his pen and be his comfort for a while."

Fury zipped right to Jen's spot and stood, trembling and snorting as his dam* walked out of the barn and onto the big stock trailer.

"Sshh, it's OK," Jen soothed, rubbing his muscled neck.

He pranced in place, not wanting to leave Jen, but not wanting to be still either. Jen spent several moments rubbing Fury's neck and shoulder.

"Movement feels like life to horses," Colton explained after he closed Sunny in the trailer. "I'll move him to another pen where he can see my other horses. He'll be all right 'til I return."

Jen climbed into the middle of the back seat of the king cab in Colton's truck. It was a little tight with Mom and Kathy. They had put their luggage in the dressing room of the trailer so there was just Mom's huge purse to contend with.

Colton returned and pulled himself into the driver's seat. "We're off!" he shouted over the rumble of the diesel engine. They crept down the driveway. Jen's stomach did flip flops waiting for the dreaded sound of a horse rearing or falling. *Please Lord, keep her safe and calm, safe and calm.* Colton turned the rig onto the road. Jen kept her eyes squeezed together. Sunny seemed fine. Jen finally allowed her eyes to flutter open. *Boy, my hands hurt,* she thought, opening them. She had deep nail prints embedded in her palms. No one else seemed even slightly concerned. Jen let out a deep sigh.

"So Colton," Mom said, leaning forward. "What time do you need to leave tomorrow?"

"I'll be dropping you folks off and drivin' back tonight," he replied looking up at her through the rear view mirror. "Need to feed my horses. My barn manager quit last month. Finally married his gal and moved."

"But that's ten hours of driving!" Mom exclaimed.

"I do it all the time when I'm on the road," Colton said as he grinned. "It's just an honest day's work."

"OK," Mom said doubtfully, settling back into her seat.

Jen flipped the magazine Kathy was reading, "What's this?" she asked.

"It's called *Jumper World*. It has some great articles, but tons of ads."

"Can I see it when you're done?"

"Here," Kathy replied, handing it to her. "I'm done. Read this article. It talks about this trainer who has such harmony with his horses that he rides without tack. His name sounds like . . . Colton Wright."

"Colton Wright!" Jen squawked. "Lemme see that!"

Sure enough, there he was on the sixth page—cowboy hat and all. Jen devoured the article. It talked about Colton's history a little, and his methods even less. The next page had a dazzling color photo of Colton and Polo jumping a four-foot picnic table, bridleless.

The following page contained a full-page advertisement for a Puissance competition. It was to be held at the Virginia Equine Showground. The grand prize was $250,000 dollars and a Mercedes Benz. It promised to attract the leading show-jumpers from around the world.

"Oohh, Mom, I want to go see this!" begged Jen. "It's in December. It can be my birthday present."

"We'll see," grinned Mom glancing at the magazine. "How do you say this word?" she asked, pointing to "puissance."

"It's pronounced pwee-sons," said Kathy. "It means high jump. I think the world record is seven feet, eight inches. They just keep raising the wall higher and higher until nobody can jump it."

"Kinda' the opposite of a limbo contest," Dad suggested from the front seat.

"Kinda'," Kathy agreed.

"Well," Jen declared passionately. "I really, really want to go see it!"

"We'll see what we can do," Dad said with a nod.

Mom's horse was bay and Dad rode a dapple-gray. Jen followed on Sunny. Mom and Dad rode so close their shoulders almost brushed together. Jen watched the valentine shaped hindquarters of the gray. They approached a clearing and continued over a little rise. There was a yellow house with black shutters, and white eyelet curtains blowing in the breeze. The yellow barn was so close it was almost attached. Where am I? Why are Mom and Dad riding?

The truck hit a bump and Jen's cheek impacted Mom's shoulder. Jen pulled herself upright. She looked around dazedly for a moment. "I had the weirdest dream," she yawned. We were all riding, even you, Dad."

"I've ridden!" he protested. "I rode every day at Colton's house."

"I told you about it, Jen," said Kathy. "I rode with your Mom and Dad. Gave them lessons and everything."

"Huh," she grunted. "I guess I remember something about it." *The yellow house, what about the yellow house?*

The maddening secret floated to the surface. "That's what I forgot!" she exclaimed. "We're losing our house. We're gonna' be homeless. Where are we going to live?" she demanded.

"Jen, settle down," Dad said, raising a surprised eyebrow at the outburst. "We have three months. We'll find a place. The Lord will provide."

"What if it's not close to Sonrise Farm?" Jen asked anxiously.

Mom put her arm around Jen's shoulder and pulled her as close as the seatbelt would allow. "Sweetheart, your Dad and I are not worried, and you shouldn't be either."

Jen relaxed against Mom and tried to put it out of her mind. It seemed the more she tried *not* to think about it, the deeper it haunted her.

Wherever it is, it's going to be too far from Sunny.

Chapter Eleven

Boy, it's good to be home. Jen stepped through the front door. The house had a warm, almost cinnamony smell. As though someone had baked snicker-doodles recently. She dropped her bags at the front door.

"Jen, you go on to the farm, Colton will drop you at the house after you get Sunny taken care of. Dad and I will stay here and start the laundry," Mom said, giving her a quick hug.

Jen scampered back to the truck and hauled herself into the front seat. Kathy had her nose buried in another horse magazine. "You guys should think about renting a horse property," she suggested.

"What!" Jenny exclaimed, horrified. "You want Sunny to leave Sonrise?"

"No silly, I was just thinking that you'd have her at home and it would be easier."

"Well," Jen huffed, "I like it right where we are, and I don't think a big change would be good for her right now. We need to get back to a normal routine."

Kathy shrugged. "It was just a suggestion."

🐎   🐎   🐎

They got Sunny settled into her old stall. The mare didn't skip a beat. Walked right in and checked out the buckets. She nudged the food bucket suggestively.

"Sorry girl, nothing in there yet," Jen apologized. "Hang on, it's coming. Here's some hay as an appetizer." Jen tossed in a flake of fragrant alfalfa, then put together a bran mash mixing in some molasses and just a handful of sweetfeed. It smelled like a combination of whole-wheat bread and oatmeal cookies. *Man, I'm hungry,* Jen realized inhaling the aroma of the mash.

Jen watched with satisfaction as Sunny began eating. "She's a dainty eater," Colton said, walking over from his self-guided tour. "You'd think, given where she's come from, that she'd wolf it down."

Jen nodded agreement. "She's always been like that, at least when she's with me."

Colton grinned at Jen. "It must mean that she's comfortable with you. You've done an amazing job with her. You two are the most connected horse/rider team I've ever seen."

Jen blushed with pleasure.

Colton continued. "I want to talk to you about Daniel."

Jen felt her heart harden at the mere mention of his name.

"Jen, you've got to forgive that boy. Not for him. For you. Forgiveness is a gift for the forgiver."

"I have forgiven him!" Jen exploded. *White hot lava.*

Colton just smiled gently, "Jen, don't forget that I lost someone precious to me too. I know how hard it is to let go. And the person I forgave last was myself. I can see the pain in your eyes."

That did it. Tears erupted out of nowhere and she was consumed by racking sobs. Colton hugged her as she cried and cried and cried. Finally, when it seemed like the barn should be flooded with tears, they stopped. Her head pounded and her nose was completely congested. Colton handed her his clean bandana. She stared at it doubtfully.

"Go ahead," he insisted. "Keep it, wash it, and bring it back when you come to pick up Fury."

She blew her nose three times, then sheepishly stuck the damp bandana into her back pocket. "I have tried to forgive him. Really I have. It's just that he's such a jerk! He still thinks you have to beat horses to get them to obey. He's unable to see how totally wrong he is."

"Didn't he *give* you Sunny and Fury?" Colton asked.

"Yes," Jen replied. "I think he did that to keep from getting in trouble. See, he knew what was going on, but he did nothing to stop it."

"And what should he have done?"

"I wanted to go to the police or the humane society or someone. He wouldn't help me."

"Did he say why?"

"Yeah, he said his Aunt V had connections with the police and that it wouldn't do any good."

"What if that's true?" Colton asked. "What if he *was* really waiting for the right time?"

"I don't know," she admitted. "He is so . . . wrong. That's it! He's wrong and won't admit it. He's clinging to what his aunt taught him."

"Maybe he needs to *see* another way," Colton suggested.

"That's just it. He has seen another way and he keeps returning to the old way."

"Jen," Colton started. "You need to forgive Daniel *and* Mrs. DuBois. You're hurting yourself by clinging to the anger. You cannot control Daniel."

"How?" she whimpered. "I've tried. It hasn't worked. The moment I think about either one, I feel this . . . anger. It feels like lava. It almost burns my throat."

"Well," he said softly, shaking his head. "Like Fury in the round pen, you'll eventually see that clinging to anger is simply an energy drain. The Lord allows us to spend our energy trying in our own strength. Eventually though, you'll see the only solution is to focus on Him. Then He is free to take your burden."

Chapter Twelve

Summer was still in full force in northern Virginia. The days were hot and sticky, the nights slightly cooler but still humid. Jen found herself longing for the crisp mountain air of Pennsylvania.

Jen sat on a hay bale in the tack room, pouring over the classifieds. *Horse property . . . 3 bedrooms, 1 1/2 baths. Barn with paddocks. $3,000.00 a month. There's no way we can afford to live here in Virginia. Not with the horses.*

School will be starting up at the end of August. Where does time go? she wondered. *I'll probably be at a different school, we'll move out of the area, I'll have to leave Kathy and Sonrise Farm.* She grew teary-eyed thinking about it.

By the time Kathy walked into the barn Jen was deep into the heartbreaking fantasy. *I'll have to sell Sunny . . .*

"What's up with you?" Kathy asked. "You look like you've lost your best friend."

"Where am I going to live?" Jen whined.

"I don't know, why are *you* worrying about this?"

"Because," Jen said, "I need to know. I need to plan. I'm probably not going to live as close to Sonrise Farm, if we even stay in this area. And what if I have to sell the horses?"

"Jen," Kathy huffed. "You are making up a story."

"What?"

"You are making up a story, imagining in your head, what might happen."

"Yeah," Jen admitted.

"Well, my dad used to say, 'Kathy, if you're going to make up a story, at least make it a good one.'" The words rolled off her tongue in perfect imitation Irish brogue.

"What does that mean?" Jen asked, smiling in spite of herself.

"It means, if you are going to sit there and imagine something, at least imagine something fabulous. It's all fantasy anyway."

"True," Jen grumped. "But how can moving be good? Things are perfect now."

Kathy pulled another hay bale over and sat. "Jen," she said seriously, "There is a God."

"I know," Jen replied impatiently.

"And you are not Him," Kathy finished.

"What does that mean?"

"It means you need to go home and read Romans 8:28."

"Right, thanks," Jen said with a sarcastic edge in her voice.

"I'm serious," Kathy warned. "No lesson tomorrow unless you can tell me what Romans 8:28 says."

Jen stalked out of the feed room carrying the buckets.

"Romans 8:28," she mumbled angrily, flitting through her Bible. "What could that possibly have to do with moving?" *There it was.*

" 'And we know that in all things God works for the good of those who love him, who have been called according to his purpose.' " Jen read the words aloud.

What does that mean, Lord? Her heart questioned.

She heard no response.

Well, at least I read it.

The lesson wasn't going well. Jen aimed Sunny at a small jump. Sunny pranced and gave a tiny rear before jigging sideways toward the eighteen-inch crossrail. Jen sat, then hauled the mare's head around to face the jump. Sunny stopped. Jen lurched forward.

"What is wrong with her today?" Jen exploded, jerking on the reins. *Is this the same horse I rode without a bridle?*

Kathy shrugged innocently. "Perhaps she doesn't like the being ridden by someone who's angry."

"I am not angry!" Jen shrieked.

Sunny reared in response.

White hot lava.

"Cut it out, you stupid mare!" Jen shouted, yanking the reins. Instantly the lava disappeared, replaced by nausea. Jen leapt off Sunny's back, "I'm sorry, Sunny. I didn't mean to . . ." Jen reached for the mare's face.

Sunny jerked her head up, her dark sensitive eyes huge with fear.

"Sunny . . . oh, what is wrong with *me?*" Jen stared helplessly at Kathy.

"Jen, I can't help you with your anger," Kathy stated matter of factly "That is a spiritual problem. I *will* take your nice mare in and untack her for you until you can get a grip. I suggest you stay off her until you work this out, unless you *want* to undo all the progress you two have made."

Coward. Abuser. Evil. The names swirled around her, accusingly. *How could I do that to my own horse?!* That question and the terror in Sunny's eyes haunted her.

"Colton," she heard herself say miserably into the phone. "I don't know what to do. Today I got really mad at Sunny and I . . ."

Silence . . .

"I . . . lost my temper. I jerked her mouth and if I'd had a crop I would have hit her."

"Are you ready to forgive Daniel and Mrs. DuBois?"

"Yes," she breathed. "I am."

"Then do it."

"How? I've tried. The anger keeps coming back."

"Well, I can tell you what has worked for me. The bottom line is that you need to realize that *you* can't do it."

"Do what?"

"Forgive Daniel and Mrs. DuBois."

"You just told me that I need to forgive them and now you're saying I can't," she huffed.

"You need to allow Jesus to forgive them through you," he replied gently. "Here's what works for me. I would ask Him to show you what *you* need to do."

Jen found herself nodding and saying "uh-huh" a lot.

She hung up and raced to her room.

"Lord, I need You to show me how to forgive Daniel and Mrs. DuBois. I am truly sick and tired of trying to carry this on my own. What do I do?"

Write.

"Write what?" she asked

Just write.

And out it came. Fifteen pages of angry questions and accusations. Anger at Dad for moving from North Carolina. *But if we hadn't moved, I would never have found Sunny.*

Anger at Daniel for not helping rescue Sunny and Fury; anger at Mrs. DuBois for hurting the horses. Anger at herself for writing to the Jockey Club for Sunny's papers. So much anger she didn't realize she harbored. More anger at Daniel for not jumping on the bandwagon of Colton's methods.

She wrote till her hand cramped. Shook it. Thought. And continued writing.

She fell asleep, pen in hand. Woke up with the sun and kept writing. When she finished, she felt clean and refreshed. *I didn't have any nightmares last night,* she realized. That dull headache she'd lived with was gone also.

Mrs. DuBois is a prisoner, Jen recognized. *Controlled by anger. The same anger I allowed into me. It's contagious. Like a disease. Lord, help Mrs. DuBois get free from anger and hatred. Oh my . . . I just prayed for Mrs. DuBois!* She chuckled out loud with joyful surprise.

I have to call Colton.

He was delighted by the call. "Come get your horse. I think you're ready for Fury to come home!"

"Are you sure?" Jen squealed.

"I was waiting on you, Jen. Not him. You weren't ready to deal with Fury. Not with that anger eating on you."

"Thank you," Jen almost whispered, suddenly humbled. "Thank you for everything."

Chapter Thirteen

"I can't wait to see Fury." Jen danced in the front seat of Kathy's truck. "And Patrick! He's home from the hospital."

"Settle down, girl," Kathy commanded, grinning. "You're shaking the whole truck."

"Oh sorry." Jen couldn't help laughing. "I'll try to sit still. I just feel so . . . free. It's like I've been sitting under a rain cloud and couldn't get out, and now it's sunny, like Sunny!" She giggled at her unintentional pun.

Even school and the impending move seemed OK. *How strange to not feel a need to know what's going to happen.*

Jen popped open the glove compartment to find more horse magazines. She leafed through the latest edition of *Sporthorse Illustrated.* Her heart skipped a beat as she flipped right to an article on the puissance competition. Four words leapt from the page: open to new competitors.

"Kathy, what does 'open to new competitors' mean in a puissance competition?"

Kathy glanced at the open page, then drew a tall drink from her bottle of spring water. "I think it means it's open to anyone. Usually puissance competitions are only open

to high point winners in A rated shows. It sounds like anyone could enter this one."

"Oh," Jen replied.

"I'll look at it again when we stop for lunch. I probably
shouldn't read and drive."

"OK!"

They pulled into the drive-through lane and ordered.
They sat in the truck and munched. "Lemme see that, Jen,"
Kathy said, taking a huge bite of biscuit. She looked closely
at the page. "There ar two ways to enter—by invitation or
qualification."

"Who invites the participants?" Jen asked.

"Usually some well-connected muckety-muck who
thinks some friend's horse has a chance. The world record
is seven foot eight. That's an amazing height," Kathy said,
shaking her head. "I've seen the puissance almost every
year at the International Horse Show. It's mind boggling."

"How would you train for that?" Jen asked.

"Mostly get the horse really fit. Then practice jumping
really big jumps. But you can't practice the big jumps too
much or you'll injure your horse. Why?"

"Just curious," Jen answered innocently.

"You're not thinking about . . . what I think you're thinking about. Are you?"

"Don't *you* think she could do it?" Jen asked, suddenly
breathless.

"Jen, you just got her back!"

"I know. But the show is four months away. We could
get her fit and then find someone to invite us."

Kathy shook her head doubtfully. "I'll help you get her
fit, but I'm not sure a puissance is a good idea. Plus, I

don't have any connections like that in the jumping world. Who will invite you?"

"Deal!" Jen hooted. "Help me get her fit. I'll figure out the rest!"

🐎 🐎 🐎

"What is Daniel's truck doing here?" Jen gasped as they pulled into Colton's driveway.

Kathy slammed her truck door closed. "Let's go see."

Colton greeted them in the kitchen, "Hey, you two," he grinned, enveloping both of them in a hug. "How was the trip?"

"Great," they harmonized.

"Hey, Colton, look at this!" Jen gushed, showing him the puissance ad. "What do you think?"

"Looks like fun," he replied, patting her back. "Are you going?"

"I want to jump Sunny in it!" she answered seriously.

His eyebrows shot up in surprise. "It's only four months away, Jen. Is that enough time to get her ready?"

"Kathy says she just needs to be super-fit. I know she can jump with the best of them."

"And what about you?" he probed. "Are you ready?"

"I'm the tick, remember?"

"And your folks?"

"I'll ask 'em. It's just that if you and Kathy won't help me, I might as well not bother. What do you say?"

Colton locked eyes with Kathy for a moment. Then he looked earnestly into Jen's eyes. "OK, here's the deal. You need to ask your parents, and we, Kathy and I, reserve the right to say 'No' at any point, even on the night of competition."

"Deal!" she agreed. "Wow, we'll be jumping with the best horses in the world!"

Colton took a deep breath. "We'll see."

"Hey, was that Daniel's truck out in your driveway?" Kathy asked.

"Yup."

"Is he here?" Kathy continued.

"Nope!" Colton replied, in an end of discussion tone of voice.

"Is Patrick here?" Jen asked.

"In the living room, watching TV and eating me out of house and home," Colton answered with a delighted grin.

"I can't wait to see him."

"Then go, and take him this juice while you're at it," he handed her a tall glass with a blue straw. "Kathy and I are gonna' put our heads together in the kitchen."

He does look better, she thought as she approached. She had expected to see a sick person, wrapped up in blankets. What she found was a thin but otherwise healthy young man dressed in jeans and a green T-shirt.

"Hi, Patrick, remember me?" She smiled and placed the juice on the pine coffee table.

"Hey, Jenny!" His clear blue eyes danced with delight.

"How do you feel?" she asked in a sing-song voice, as if she were talking to a three-year-old.

"I feel incredible," he answered, beaming. "There's still a little pain at the incision site, but that's almost nothing. To be home and not worried about my next dialysis appointment feels like heaven!"

Jen felt a stab of guilt. For being healthy and taking it for granted. For not wanting to donate a kidney to this young man. "I'm so glad you're doing well," she said sincerely. "I've been praying for you."

"Thanks," he replied. "Hey. Is Daniel back yet?"

"I haven't seen him."

"Drat, he's picking up our pizza. I'm starving."

Jen walked slowly to the kitchen. *I can't believe that is the same guy I saw last month. He looked like he was dying. I guess he was dying. And now, he's waiting for pizza!*

Colton's little Toyota stopped in the driveway with a lurch. Daniel slid out from the driver's seat then reached back in to extract a gigantic pizza box. He carried it high over his head like a French waiter. Jen saw him look hard at Kathy's truck before waltzing in the back door.

"Hi there, long time no see," he greeted, sliding past them. "I'd stay and chat but I have this custom-made, extra-super-large, four-cheese pizza with mushrooms and black olives calling Patrick's and my names. I'll come back in and catch up with you later."

Kathy and Jen exchanged confused glances.

"He's been just wonderful," Colton exclaimed.

"What's he doing here?" Jen asked.

"Helpin' out," Colton said with a shrug. "He's been great company for Patrick. They're like brothers."

"Be careful," Jen warned, feeling a prickling sensation on the back of her neck. "He doesn't share your ideas, Colton. I hope he hasn't been near Fury."

"Actually Jen, he's been helping me with Fury," Colton shared. "He's coming along."

Jen's mouth hung open in shock. "How could you!" she breathed. "Fury is terrified of him."

"Not any more he's not," Colton responded gently. "I thought you forgave Daniel and his aunt."

"I did! I didn't expect to have to see him again . . . so soon." Now her face was heating up, her eyes stinging. *No! No crying.*

"Well, Jen," Colton said softly. "Here's where the rubber meets the road."

"What does that mean?" Jen huffed indignantly.

"It means, here's where you see who's strength *you* rely on. If you forgive in your strength, it is meaningless. If you forgive in His strength, it is permanent."

"What do you mean?" Jen sobbed bitterly, feeling confused.

Colton stood up and placed his burly arm around her shoulders. He smelled like horse sweat and pine shavings. "Jen, do you trust me?"

"Yes," she replied nodding her head.

"Will you trust me even though this looks wrong to you?"

She stared at him for several moments, studying his weathered face. His eyes were kind with lots of smile wrinkles around them.

Her shoulders sagged. "Yes," she sighed. "I do trust you, even though it looks wrong to me."

"I should tell you that Dan hasn't been able to do much *yet*. He's been watching and learning. He needs to be careful."

"Why does he need to be careful?" she questioned.

"Because he's recovering . . . from donating a kidney . . . to my son."

Chapter Fourteen

Daniel donated his kidney. Unbelievable. I really thought he was a total coward. She was still shaking her head as she climbed into the comfy twin bed in the blue guestroom. This room had twin beds and a private bath. Kathy climbed in the other bed and punched the squishy pillow until it was just right.

"Can you believe Daniel gave his kidney to Patrick?" Jen whispered.

"Yeah, I believe it," Kathy nodded.

"It's amazing," Jen continued.

"Well, maybe Daniel is not who you thought he was," Kathy suggested.

"Maybe," Jen agreed, turning over. "Maybe."

Colton and Kathy went over the written plan for Sunny's conditioning program. Jen sat at the end of the kitchen table watching through the bay windows as Daniel interacted with Fury. The colt was not fearful of him, just as Colton had said.

Colton glanced up and noticed Jen watching the horse and young man. "He's made incredible strides, Jen. They both have. Fury really enjoys Daniel and Daniel truly wants to understand Fury. It's a beautiful thing to watch."

Jen stepped outside to have a closer look. Fury stood watching Dan intently. Dan took off jogging, the colt stayed at his side. Dan stopped suddenly, the colt screeched on the brakes. Dan took off again, Fury followed. Jen got goosebumps watching them. They were having fun! Playing. The connection between the two was undeniable. *Fury wants to be with Daniel!*

Leave him here.

Leave Fury? With Colton and Dan? We just drove five hours to get him! What do I tell Kathy?

Leave him with Daniel.

Jen walked dazedly into the kitchen. "Kathy, I think I should leave Fury here."

Kathy's eyes grew wide. "Leave him? Here? With Daniel here?"

"Hallelujah!" Colton whooped. "I hoped you would do that. I can't tell you what that colt has meant to that boy."

Jen shrugged helplessly at Kathy's shocked expression. "I know it sounds crazy, but He's telling me to do it." She pointed up.

"OK," Kathy replied. "We don't argue with Him."

Jen's gaze traveled outside to the round pen. Doubt still gnawed at her heart. *What if Daniel's just fooling everyone? What if he's just waiting to get his hands on Fury when Colton's not around? What if Mrs. DuBois calls and talks him into . . . who knows?* "It's you I'm trusting, Colton, not Daniel," she said, more sharply than she meant to.

Colton looked up from the table. "OK," he replied softly. "I'll take responsibility for Fury and Daniel."

Lord, I trust You. You told me to leave Fury here. I'm leaving him here in Your care.

You can trust Me, Jen.

Kathy and Jen brushed their teeth after breakfast, said their goodbyes and headed back to Virginia. "Well, that was a wasted trip," Jen remarked, climbing into the cab and clicking the seat belt.

"No it wasn't," Kathy squawked. "You found out about the puissance, convinced Colton to help you with what will probably be the biggest jumping competition *you've* ever done, and you got to see that Daniel is doing all right. I think we did a lot on this trip."

"You're right," Jen agreed. "I guess I was focusing on moving Fury home and we didn't do that, but you're right. We did other stuff. Now we've got five hours to figure out how to convince my folks to let Sunny and me jump. We probally won't make it to the finals, but that's fine. I just want a chance!"

They pulled up in Jen's driveway and sat for a moment. They still hadn't come up with any particularly convincing reasons for doing the puissance competition.

Jen stared at Kathy. "Anything?"

"Nope," Kathy shrugged. "Let's just go ask 'em."

"Can we pray first?" Jen requested.

"Great idea. You go."

"Dearest Lord Jesus, You know how this turns out. Please help me ask my folks."

Kathy stared at Jen, surprised, for a moment, then smiled. "Thank You, Lord, that You do know everything. Thank You for Jenny. We trust that You will do what is best for her."

"Amen," they chorused.

"I really expected you to ask Him to help you *convince* your parents," Kathy whispered on the way to the back door.

"Mom and Dad," Jen called from the tiny kitchen.

"Hey, Sweetie," Dad called back. "We're down here, in the basement."

Jen walked cautiously down the rickety wood stairs. "What are you doing down here?"

"Going through stuff for the move. We still have boxes we haven't unpacked from the first move."

The move! I forgot about the move! I am not going to worry about the move, she decided. "I need to ask you guys something," she announced confidently.

"Great," Dad replied. "I need a tall glass of something anyway. "Come on, Mom."

They sat around the kitchen table with lemonade. Jen showed them the ad in the magazine again. "See this," she pointed to the sentence: " 'Competition, by invitation.' This means that Sunny and I could *compete* in this. I really, really want to. I know we probably won't make it past the first jump off but I want to try. Colton and Kathy said they'd help."

Dad reached for his lemonade and took a long drink. Jen heard the kitchen clock marking time, loud, louder, louder.

"What are the details?" Dad finally asked.

"I'm not sure," Jen shrugged. "I wanted to ask your permission before I got information."

Dad's face beamed. "I'm impressed. Get the details. Mom and I will discuss it and we'll all meet back here in three days at this time. Sound fair?"

"Fair!" she agreed. "I'll call the 800 number right now!"

"You have reached the International Puissance information line," the recording assured her. "If you are calling for ticket information please press one now. For a complete listing of sponsors, please press two now. For directions to the arena, please press three now. For an application to compete, please press four now."

She pressed four and recited her address to the automated voice.

"Now I get to hurry up and wait," she grumped, feeling very unsatisfied.

The application arrived. It was almost a work of art in itself. Eight and a half by eleven, glossy paper, with photos of horses sailing over jumps. *Gorgeous,* thought Jen feeling her heart pick up speed at the thought of being airborne over a jump with Sunny. She cradled the application gently. It seemed a shame to write on it.

"Name of horse," read Jen out loud. "Hmm, I wonder which name I should use? Her Jockey Club name or the name I gave her?" She decided on Endless Sonrise. Jen's fingers flew.

"Names and dates of rated shows. Can't answer that one. Name of invitational sponsor. Now what? We don't have any rated shows under our belt, and no 'invitational sponsor.' " Then she remembered. *The recording. The recording had a list of sponsors.*

She punched the phone number again. This time she pressed number two for a listing of sponsors. Sponsor number one made her take the phone off her ear and hang up in a daze.

The DuBois Farm? The main sponsor of the International Puissance is Vanessa DuBois?!

It felt like someone had punched her in the stomach.

Chapter Fifteen

"What should I do?" Jen moaned into the phone.

"Call Daniel," Kathy suggested. "Maybe he can pull some strings with his Auntie V."

"You don't understand. Sunny won't jump if that woman is anywhere near her. She'll freak out and . . . well, it won't be good."

"Call Daniel and tell Colton what's going on. It's the only chance you have. It's that or give up on this competition."

Call.

She dialed Colton's number. "Please don't answer, please don't answer," she pleaded quietly.

"Hello, Wright's," answered Daniel's voice.

Jen grimaced. "Hi, Daniel," she chirped. *Do I sound as fake as I feel?* She wondered.

"Hey, girl," he greeted, sounding genuinely pleased.

"Do you know anything about this puissance competition?" she asked casually.

His heavy sigh told her the answer. "Yeah, but I wish I didn't. Aunt Vanessa asked me to help her with the competition."

"Help! How?"

"She's looking for her next jumper prospect, Jen. She's got the bucks to buy any horse in the world. Except now she can't legally own one, because of her cruelty conviction. She asked me to be the legal owner of the new horse and 'board' at her place."

Jen gasped out loud. "What did you say?"

"I said 'No,' of course."

"How can I get Sunny and me into this competition?"

Silence. "Why would you want to do this competition with Sunny of all horses?"

"Because I want her to have a chance to prove herself," Jen spouted passionately. "We just want a chance."

"OK, OK," he replied. "I'll see what I can do. I think you're crazy, though."

"Thank you, Daniel," she responded gratefully.

Lord, give me patience, she pleaded. *Waiting is the worst!* She stalked into her bedroom. Her Bible sat on the desk inviting her with open pages. She sidled over to it. Isaiah 40:31 jumped out at her.

Come.

She sighed . . .

"Those who hope in the LORD will renew their strength. They will soar on wings like eagles; they will run and not grow weary, they will walk and not be faint."

I get it, she smiled. *Thank You.*

The tri-fold invitation form arrived in the mailbox. It was so plain looking it almost looked like junk mail. Jen tried to open it without tearing it. It had a Xeroxed signature at the bottom. Vanessa DuBois. She stared at the name like it was a large hairy spider. *It gives me the willies,* she thought with a shudder.

She filled the form out quickly, using Endless Sonrise as Sunny's name. An envelope, a stamp, and it was back in the mailbox with the flag up.

We'll wait and see what happens.

Sunny was in fine form. Her glossy neck arched as she trotted powerfully around the ring. It was like riding a locomotive. Jen sat and relaxed her seat, asking the big mare to slow to a walk. Sunny slowed gradually. Jen finally used the reins.

"Slow down, girl," Jen crooned. "There's no hurry."

Sunny snorted but responded to the gentle pull on the bit.

"Keep asking her with your body first," Kathy instructed. "Use the reins when you have to. She'll figure it out. Let's do some little jumps, then go for a trail ride."

The weather was grand. It was slightly breezy which kept the flies at bay, and sunny but not humid. One of those days when it just felt good to be alive. Kathy was on Magnum. He looked great too. Glossy dark coat, ears pricked forward.

They walked the perimeter of the fence surrounding Sonrise Farm. Jen practiced using her seat to ask Sunny to speed up, then slow down, then speed up, then . . . *I have the strangest feeling—like I've been here before.*

"I'm having déjà vu—you know, the feeling that I've been here before," she mentioned to Kathy.

"Really? I don't think I've ever taken you back here."

They were suddenly out of the trees and in a glade. A bedraggled cottage stood at the far end. *It looks so familiar.* Then she remembered. *I've dreamed about this house. This is the place where Mom and Dad are riding with me.*

Jen's lungs filled with air involuntarily. "What is this place?" she breathed.

"This used to be the main house," Kathy said with a shrug. "My folks built the big house when I was born. This house has been used as a guesthouse or as a spare housing for the employees. It needs some work. My dad's been talking about renting it out again, but it really needs to be painted, inside and out."

"What about us? Could we rent it?" Jen asked.

"You wouldn't want to rent it. It's tiny and needs a ton of work."

"Would you ask your dad?" Jen persisted.

"Sure," Kathy sighed, rolling her eyes.

Jen leaned forward and rubbed Sunny's neck. "Let's go back and muck so I can get home," she suggested, suddenly anxious to talk to her parents.

Dad sounded mildly interested in at least seeing it, Mom, not even slightly.

"It sounds even smaller than this house," she explained. "We're cramped *here*. I can't possibly go smaller. Nope." She shook her head emphatically, just in case anyone harbored any doubts.

I was so sure, Jen thought.

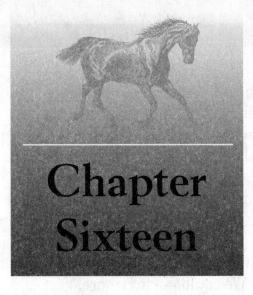

Chapter Sixteen

"Jen," Mom said casually at breakfast. "How would you like to homeschool?"

"You mean do school at home?" she gasped.

"Yes," Mom nodded, smiling. "School at home."

"You mean, no school bus, no lunch line, no bells?"

Mom kept nodding.

Jen's mind went blank. *Wonderful! Incredible!*

"Mom," she breathed. "That would be wonderful, incredible. I've gotta' call Kathy!"

"The down side is I'd like to start now," Mom explained. "*Before* the county does, because we're going to be moving . . . somewhere . . . I'd like to get a head start, cause we're going to need your help with the move."

"Whatever you say," Jen saluted crisply, exhilarated by a sudden sense of freedom.

🐎 🐎 🐎

"Man, you're lucky!" Kathy squawked. "You get to be home, or here . . . mucking . . . so I can ride . . . Yes! This has possibilities!" She rubbed her chin, twisting her face in her best impression of a slave driver.

"Yeah, right," Jen said in a disgusted voice. "*My* PE will definitely be horsebackriding. And we still don't know where we're going."

"It'll be nearby," Kathy said reassuringly. "Your dad's business is going well. He's not gonna' move you guys too far away."

"That's just it, Kathy. He's got contracts all over the East Coast. We could go anywhere!"

"Fortunately," Kathy reminded, "we know the Sovereign Lord of the universe and He has everything under control."

For I know the plans I have for you, plans for good, not evil.

Jen could only smile gratefully. "It's true."

"Now, let's get you on that gorgeous mare of yours and get ready for the puissance!"

What is it about jumping that you love, Sunny? Jen wondered as they sailed over an oxer. The mare's ears were forward, her dark eyes revealing a sense of fun. "You are just having fun, aren't you, girl?" Jen touched the reins ever so slightly to ask for a halt. She rubbed the powerful neck releasing the reins at the same time. Sunny heaved a contented sigh and cocked a back leg.

"I've never seen a horse who loved jumping like this one." Kathy grinned as she spoke, walking over from the center of the ring. "Her eyes positively glow as she goes over."

"I know," Jen agreed.

"Well, she's earned her dinner tonight. Let's cool her off and get her fed."

Jen walked with Sunny, lead rope draped over her mighty back. Jen stopped, Sunny stopped. Jen walked, Sunny walked. Jen stopped, then picked up her left foot and waited. Sunny mimicked perfectly. Other side. Same game. Same harmony.

It's breathtaking she realized. *To have a horse want to be with you. To want to be close. To want to obey, simply out of love and trust.*

It's the same for Me, Jen. I want harmony, obedience, closeness. I only want it if it's born of love and trust.

Trust. Love. Closeness. I want those too, Lord.

I love you, Jennifer Lynne. Beyond measure. And Sunny too. It is I who gives Sunny her love for jumping. It is I who gives you your passion for horses. These are my gifts to you to help you understand My love.

Jen stopped in her tracks. Tears poured unnoticed down her face. She was overwhelmed by deep knowledge. *God loves me. He loves me like I love Sunny!*

Sunny's warm breath brought Jen back to her senses. A mighty dam burst in Jen's soul, loosing an endless ocean of love. Everything, even the barn around her looked new.

She wrapped her arms around Sunny's neck and hugged. The big mare leaned into the embrace. Inexpressible joy filled and overflowed Jen's heart.

She could only whisper, "Thank You, thank You, thank You, Lord."

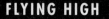

The change permeated every aspect of Jen's life. *How strange that I'm not worried about where we are going to live or the puissance or Fury. All the things I thought I should worry about. This is freedom. This is peace.*

Jen's mind floated back to a conversation with Colton from the summer. "Anything He wants to do *for* me or to me, through me, by me, or about me is OK with me. I know He is doing them all for my best. No matter how it looks to anyone else, including myself."

Jen smiled remembering the sparkle in Colton's eyes as he spoke. Colton had said those words as Patrick lay dying, waiting for his new kidney. *Colton had totally surrendered.* Thinking of Patrick caused Jen to ponder her own body. Her heartbeat. Her ability to breathe. *All are from You, Lord.*

I gave you a heartbeat and a need to breathe so you would be reminded of Me, always. I am with you always. As steady as a heartbeat.

Jen lifted her face skyward. *This is what they mean by Amazing Grace!*

Chapter Seventeen

"Hey, Jen." It was Daniel's voice on the other end of the phone. "The puissance is a couple of months away. I thought I should warn you of some things. I convinced Aunt Vanessa to let you guys jump by reminding her that Sunny's likely to freak out when she smells and sees her. I should tell you where Aunt V plans to sit, and I have some clothes of hers. I thought you could use them to get Sunny desensitized to her smell. She wears this nasty perfume and *I* can still smell it on the shirt. You should also know that she will stop at almost nothing to discredit you. She is looking forward to showing the horse world that Sunny is a dangerous animal. This puissance is the biggest thing on the East Coast."

"OK," Jen said, not knowing what else to say. "I'm not worried, Daniel. The Lord is with me, I'm not worried about your aunt, or how many people will be there."

"Suit yourself," he replied. "Colton wants to talk to your folks about something. Is your dad there?"

"Nope, he's at a job site. He should be home for lunch

soon. Wait, you can call him on his cell phone." She read the number to him."

"Thanks, Jen. I'll see you soon."

"Are you coming to the puissance?" she asked.

"Wouldn't miss it," he replied. She could hear the grin in his voice.

"Pack up, Jen. We're going to Colton's," Mom announced an hour later.

"What?" Jen sputtered, looking up from the history of Spain.

"Pack up," Mom repeated. "You, Sunny, Kathy and I are going to Colton's."

"What about Dad?" Jen asked, totally shocked.

"He's busy with a big job right now. Come on, I want to get there by dark. You can finish your school work in the truck."

Jen leapt from her chair to throw the necessaries in a small, blue duffel bag.

I sure love homeschooling she thought to herself. *There's no way I could do this otherwise.* She leaned forward to squeeze Mom gently around the neck. "Thanks for everything," she said softly.

"Are you buckled up?" Mom asked, rubbing Jen's arm.

"Yes."

She glanced behind her into the stock trailer. She could still see Sunny in the fading light. The mare jerked a large wad of hay from the hay net and began chewing.

She's fine.

They pulled into Cedar Woods right after dark.

"How's the house hunt coming?" Colton inquired over Chinese food.

"Haven't found anything yet," Mom said with a shrug. "Mike's got all his feelers out. Something will turn up."

"You can always move in here," Colton offered.

"Thanks." Mom smiled and reached for the lo mein. "I'll tell Mike and we'll keep that in mind."

That would be awesome! Jen thought. *I could be Colton's new apprentice!*

The month of November flew by. Jen spent hours in the saddle on Sunny, Polo, and Colton's other horses. There were plenty of hills to trot up and down to strengthen Sunny's already powerful hindquarters. Sunny and Jen were clearing five feet two inches without any trouble. "It feels weird to set up a jump higher than my head," Jen called to Kathy.

"That jump is still two feet shorter than what you guys need to clear to make it through the first round. We'll keep doing what we're doing. The most important thing to do right now is trot, trot, trot. That'll get her fit. We'll jump once a week."

Dad drove up for the Thanksgiving weekend. "I've missed my girls," he said, squeezing them both in a tremendous bear hug.

"How's it going, Mike?" Mom asked.

"Well," Dad said, "I've moved all our stuff into a storage facility and I'm staying with Pastor Jeff."

"You were careful with the china, of course."

"Of course!" Dad replied.

"So we're homeless?" Jen asked.

"Uh, yeah, I guess we are," he admitted.

"It's going to be all right, Jen. You don't need to worry," Mom said.

"I'm not worried at all." Jen grinned. "It's kind of exciting to see where we wind up."

"That's my girl," Dad beamed. "You're so right!"

December 15. The puissance. Two weeks away. Are we ready? she wondered as she crossed another day off the calendar. She ambled downstairs to check out breakfast. *Boy it's quiet for 7:00 A.M. Where is everyone?*

Colton's horses gathered impatiently by the gate whickering and jostling for position. Jen grabbed an apple and headed outside to start feeding.

Daniel arrived at the barn halfway through. "Sorry," he puffed. "Colton's really sick with the flu or something." They finished feeding together, then walked in the back door to find Kathy sitting at the table staring vacantly out the window.

"I want to help, really I do," she moaned. "I feel like someone is beating on my head with a baseball bat."

"Go back to bed," Daniel commanded. "We don't want your germs down here. Colton's sick too."

Kathy nodded weakly and slumped back upstairs.

"Great," Daniel said. "Now what? If this is the flu I had, it'll be a good two weeks before they're any use to anybody."

"I don't know," Jen admitted. 'We'll just pray that they feel better soon."

Daniel rolled his eyes. "You all sure do pray a lot. I don't see the point."

Jen opened her mouth to snap at him.

Stop. He does not know Me.

Daniel glanced her way, clearly expecting harsh words.

She smiled kindly. "Prayer does work Dan. But it only works because of who we're praying to." *It's weird, I open my mouth and words come out. Words that don't sound like mine, but are.*

"Whatever," he shrugged. "I'll help you with Sunny, if you want."

Jen stared at his earnest face. "I don't think that's a good idea."

"OK," he mumbled, looking hurt. "I need to muck out. Later."

Jen felt torn. *What do I do Lord? I don't trust him.*

You know what to do, Jen. Trust Me. And let Daniel help you.

She marched to the barn to help with stalls. "Daniel?" she began.

"What," he replied gruffly.

"Can you help me after we finish the barn?"

"Sure!"

🐎   🐎   🐎

Daniel carried his aunt's clothes into the huge indoor arena. He dumped them in the corner and wandered over to where Sunny stood. The mare nuzzled his pockets for treats. Dan stared at the big horse. "She looks great, Jen. I feel like Aunt Vanessa's place was in a different life. I'm so glad Sunny's forgiven me. Being Colton's apprentice has sure changed my way of thinking."

"You're Colton's apprentice?" Jen squawked.

"Yup," Daniel replied. "Patrick and I are doing the apprenticeship together. I'm on the family scholarship plan."

"What's that?" Jen asked.

"Evidently, if you donate an organ to this family they adopt you . . . sort of. Colton says he now has two sons. It's amazing Jen. I always wanted a family who cared. I used to pray for a dad who loved me . . . when I was little. God never heard my prayer."

"He's *answered* your prayer now!" Jen declared.

"A little late," Dan stated bitterly.

" 'And we know that in all things God works for the good of those who love him, who have been called according to his purpose,' Romans 8:28. You should memorize that verse, Daniel. It'll help you."

Daniel just looked at her. "Do you want me to help you jump or do you want to sit here preaching at me?"

"Let's jump," Jen agreed.

Sunny cleared six feet easily.

Chapter Eighteen

Colton groaned and rolled over. Jen stayed at the doorway, afraid to get too close. "Daniel can help you, Jen. Give him a chance. He's really changed."

"He *is* helping me," Jen replied. "Sunny and I just cleared six feet."

"Yeah," Colton cheered. The cheer interrupted by a severe coughing spell. "You three can do this!" he whispered after it passed.

She nodded and headed back out to ride Polo.

"Right there, that's where he made the change!" Daniel's face revealed his joy.

"I didn't see it," Jen complained, stuffing more popcorn into her mouth. They had viewed the video of Colton and Fury many times. Now even Daniel was able to see that miraculous moment when Fury *chose* to be with Colton.

"OK," Daniel sighed patiently. "Let's watch it again."

This time she just watched. She didn't squint her eyes or try to concentrate. She just watched. *Lord, help me see that moment*. And there it was. It was nothing amazing, yet it was incredible. It was simply the moment the big colt *decided* to trust Colton. *You allow us to run around Lord, to try all our options. It always comes back to You. You are the source of everything good. But You patiently allow us decide to be with You.*

It brought tears to Jen's eyes and goose bumps to her arms. "Thank You," she murmured out loud.

"You're welcome," Daniel answered.

She grinned at him.

The puissance is in two days. Sunny's fit, I'm fit, we haven't cleared seven feet but that's because there aren't any jumps high enough around here.

I know we can do it. We just need a chance.

Colton and Kathy were feeling better. The hacking cough lingered making sleep difficult, but at least the fever was gone.

"You guys are doing great!" Colton enthused, watching Jen and Sunny. He walked over to rub the mare's neck. "Man, I should just go back to bed, you don't need me. It would be helpful if you played some loud music. Get her used to the sounds of being inside. Screaming and clapping would be good too. We'll teach her that those sounds mean 'hurry up and relax.'"

Daniel worked the boom box. Colton stood at Sunny's shoulder. Dan found a rock station, cranked the volume, and hit the 'on' button. Squealing guitar tones burst from the radio. Sunny startled, but stood, dancing in place. Colton placed his hand on her poll and gave her the 'head down' cue. As soon as her head dropped a fraction Dan hit the 'off' button. After three times, Sunny took the tortured screaming guitar sounds as a 'head down' cue. She stood quietly licking her lips.

"She's chewing on that thought," Colton grinned. We'll do the same with applause sounds. But we'll do that tomorrow. I *do* need to go back to bed now."

Do it now. The thought was persistent. Jen tried arguing. *But Lord, he hurt me and Sunny.*

How did Daniel hurt you?

He wouldn't help me save Sunny and Fury.

He did save them.

Yeah, but almost too late.

If it were not for Daniel, you would not have Sunny.

Unthinkable.

Ask Daniel about Sunny. About how she wound up with the cows.

"Hey, Daniel," Jen said after dinner. They sat in front of the crackling fire in the great room.

"Hey what?" he asked.

"Do you know how Sunny wound up in the cow field?"

He stared at her intently. "Why?" he asked suspiciously. "Who wants to know?"

"Me, I want to know."

There was a long hesitation. Daniel stared at his hands, studying the palms. "I put her there," he murmured.

"What?!"

"She was almost starved to death. She wouldn't have lasted another week. I coated her in mud and walked her to the field. I prayed the farmer would feed her or at least leave her alone to eat the grass. I didn't know what else to do. Aunt Vanessa hated her and wanted her dead. It looked like it had worked out for everyone. Sunny was out of Aunt V's clutches, Aunt V had the insurance money, and I didn't have to see Sunny in pain anymore."

"You mean *you* rescued her from your aunt?"

He hesitated again. "Yeah, I guess that's what I did." He nodded thoughtfully. "And if someone hadn't been so gung-ho about knowing her blood lines, we could have avoided the whole mountain scene."

Jen stared at him in disbelief. "Daniel, look at where we are! That whole 'mountain scene' brought us here. I *own* Sunny and Fury. Your aunt will never have them again. *You* are apprenticing with the greatest horse trainer on the face of the earth."

Jen stood and gazed up into the massive oak bookcase. She spied and grabbed a huge leather-bound Bible. Her fingers flew to the now familiar Romans 8:28 and read aloud, " 'And we *know* that in all things God works for the good of those who love him, who have been called according to his purpose' " (emphasis supplied).

"Daniel, we don't need to worry about the stuff that happens. He's the God. He has it under control. Even the terrible and evil stuff is *used* by Him and turned into good."

Daniel's face twisted in pain. "I'd like to believe that, really I would. I just can't. I have prayed so many times and never had an answer. I can't believe."

I feel so sad for him, she realized. *I've been getting mad at him for not seeing truth. But he really wants to see. He wants to choose.*

"Well," she went on, clearing her throat. "I need to ask your forgiveness."

"What?" He looked startled.

She gulped. "I've been really angry at you. For not helping me save Sunny; for lots of things. I am truly sorry, and I'm asking you to forgive me."

Daniel stared at her, eyes questioning. "Uh, yeah sure, I forgive you. Don't worry about it." He shrugged, trying to look casual. "Nobody ever asked me to forgive them before," he mumbled.

Jealousy, Pride, Anger. All vanished.

Jen breathed an audible sigh of relief. The last vestiges of pain swirled away from her. *Amazing Grace.* The old hymn filled her mind. It felt like it was bursting from her. She hummed a few bars.

Chapter Nineteen

The puissance. It's tomorrow! The day I've been waiting for. She scrambled into some sweats and headed downstairs. *Daddy's coming this afternoon. Haven't seen him since Thanksgiving. Gotta' finish school early so I can get ready.*

Nobody else stirred as she moused her way through the house, headed to the great room. Daniel sat hunched and focused in front of the TV. He was watching and rewinding and re-watching a video of Fury and Colton.

"What are you doing?" Jen asked, mystified.

"Nothin'," he muttered, clearly embarrassed.

"Really," she inquired gently, "what are you doing?"

"I was noticing that Fury lost his fear when he focused all his attention on Colton. See here? His eyes are still fearful, but here, this moment, he chooses Colton and peace comes."

Jen nodded understanding.

"Colton says," Daniel continued, "that God pursues us the same way he pursues horses. With love and patience. Fury's not worried about any other horse. He's not struggling anymore. He's only looking at Colton. That's where peace is. I want peace, Jen. I'm tired. I'm tired of hating my aunt, tired of being mad at my dad. I'm tired."

Daniel's eyes reflected the same hopeless look many horses have. Jen sat down next to him. "Jesus is my peace," she murmured. "He's your peace too, if you'll have Him."

"What do I do?" Daniel whispered. "I want what you have. I want to know . . ."

He stopped, unable to go on. Years of pain and struggle leapt forward in his eyes.

"Daniel. You just ask. Would you like me to pray with you?"

He nodded his head.

"Dearest Lord Jesus," she began. "Thank You for dying for my sins. Thank You for Your resurrection and the life it gives to me."

Daniel repeated what she said.

"I am ready to turn from my sins and come to You."

He repeated again.

"Thank You for eternal life and a new life here on earth."

He repeated the last sentence. His eyes fluttered open and Jen witnessed that same miraculous moment she'd seen on tape with Fury. That fleeting recognition and release followed by peace.

She smiled gently at him. "Welcome to the family. I always wanted a brother."

He grinned shyly. "Thanks, sis."

Dad arrived at 2:00. He burst through the kitchen door. "I'm here!" he shouted.

Jen flew across the room to greet him. "Daddy!" she shrieked, grabbing him.

"Whew, are you getting strong," he groaned. "You're gonna' squash me."

"I missed you and missed you," she complained. "How's that big project coming?"

He winked and grinned. "Almost done!"

"Will you come and stay here when you finish?"

"No," he replied casually. "We'll all go back home."

"Home! What do you mean home?"

"You know, back in Northern Virginia."

"Dad?" she probed suspiciously. "Where are we going to stay?"

"Something'll turn up," he answered with a laugh. "Where's Mom?"

Jen grinned and pointed. "She's helping out in the barn."

Dad looked shocked. "The barn, as in mucking out the stalls?"

"Yeah, she's really good."

Dad shook his head, then turned and walked out the door toward the barn. Jen ran upstairs to pack her britches and boots for the puissance. *Tomorrow.*

🐎 🐎 🐎

The World International Arena was overwhelming. The lights, the noise, the sheer size of the place. Empty, it looked cavernous. Full it would look . . . terrifying. Indoor seating for 80,000 people. Jen could only gawk.

They found an empty stall and got Sunny comfortably settled in. Someone would be with her at all times . . . just in case. "What do ya' think, girl?" Jen crooned as they walked in. *I wonder what you'll think of tonight?* The mare's dark eyes were calm and trusting. Jen brushed her for a few minutes, not because she needed it but because Jen needed it.

Sunny's nose came around to nuzzle Jen softly. "You are my sunshine, my only sunshine. You make me happy when skies are gray. You'll never know dear, how much I love you. Please don't take my sunshine away," Jen sang then hummed. Sunny's ears swiveled around listening as Jen deftly brushed.

You'll never know dear . . . how much I love you.

The words echoed over and over in Jen's spirit. *Thank You, Lord. I love You too.*

She breathed deeply and giggled to hear Sunny sigh at the same time.

Daniel bounded over full of news. "Jen! You won't believe it! I just saw reporters from Russia! This is the biggest horse event in the history of show-jumping! The guy I talked to said it will be televised worldwide . . . live! All the major stations are showing it."

Jen gulped, feeling her blood pressure climb.

You'll never know dear . . . how much I love you.

Jen grinned. "This gigantic stadium full of people is very small compared to You, Lord. I know the Lord of the universe. Why should I be scared of a bunch of people?"

Daniel raised his eyebrows. "You talk to Him like you know Him, Jen. How do you do that?"

"I don't know. I just talk and then I listen. The more I listen, the easier it is to hear Him."

He shook his head, then asked, "Are you ready? I'll help you tack up."

Suddenly, as she mounted, reality struck again. *80,000 people. Live simulcast coverage. People in far away places hunched over the TV.* Butterflies, really big, hairy ones flew in and out of her stomach.

Sunny danced as Jen got stiff.

"Don't forget to breathe!" Daniel shouted from across the warm up ring.

"Oh yeah, that." She exhaled and forced her muscles to relax. Sunny stopped dancing. "Sorry, girl," Jen apologized as she rubbed her glossy neck. "I'm making you nervous."

The warm up area was small and getting dusty. Horses reared and bucked in place in excitement. Jen trotted Sunny around and around to warm her up. She didn't feel a need to jump any of the practice jumps. She noted several world famous riders. Some riders stared at her, as if wondering where she'd come from. She smiled back and waved cheerfully. That was usually enough to make them duck their heads and look elsewhere.

"I guess I'm not the run of the mill pro rider, Sunny," she murmured.

An attractive blond reporter edged her way around the perimeter of the ring. She tried talking to some of the riders but they held up their hands in warning. One of the horses actually cow-kicked as she tried to approach. The young woman looked up at Jen, flushed and frustrated. Her look quickly changed to curiosity as she searched Jen's face.

She walked over toward Sunny cautiously. "Are you a competitor?" she asked.

Jen nodded.

The reporter inched closer. "I've never seen you or your horse before. This puissance is full of the top riders in the world. What are you doing here?"

"I'm jumping," Jen said calmly, as if it were a normal occurrence.

The reporter pulled out her little pad hungrily just as Jen heard her name over the loudspeaker.

"I'm sorry, I have to go," Jen apologized.

"Jennifer Lynn Thomas," the reporter repeated after the loudspeaker, watching the girl on the gold mare.

Jen guided Sunny up the ramp toward the arena. The lights were blinding. *Don't look up there. Keep your eyes on the ring. Breathe. Relax.*

The jump was huge. Seven feet tall. It looked absolutely unjumpable. Jen's heart dropped. *What was I thinking? We can't do this!*

I will give you wings like eagles.

What?

Sunny jumped seven feet to get out of her pen.

That's right! I'd forgotten that was seven feet.

Jen trotted Sunny to the far end of the arena. She focused her eyes on the jump. Leaned forward, gave the mare a tiny squeeze, Sunny exploded into a powerful canter. Closer. Closer. It looked like they were going to collide with it. Jen fought the desire to close her eyes and hang on. *I've got to do this with her. We're a team.* Take off.

Sunny launched as if from a cannon. Up. Up. Up. That heart-catching moment at the top. Then landing. Jen pitched forward, losing a stirrup in the process. She grabbed the pommel of the saddle to balance herself.

A glance behind them. The top layer of bricks stayed up! They were clear!

Sunny snorted the sand dust from her nostrils as they walked toward the warm up area.

Twelve more riders to go. Five horses knocked a brick down and were eliminated. The wall was raised to 7'4".

"Come on Sunny, our turn."

This time Jen didn't see anything but the wall.

She rode to the far end of the arena. Turned and gave a tiny squeeze. Beautiful transition into a canter. Wait. Wait. Now! Jen stood in the stirrups and threw the reins forward to allow Sunny full neck stretch. This time it felt like a high-speed elevator. Up forever.

They landed smoothly. No bricks down. Clean again.

They lost six more riders at 7'4".

Now it was Jen on Sunny, the tall thin English guy on a bay, and Margie something on a big gray.

The wall was raised to 7'6".

Jen sat on Sunny who cocked a back leg and looked almost dozy. The air was heating up and someone cracked a door to allow cold air to enter. Jen moved Sunny away from the draft.

"Jennifer Lynn Thomas and Endless Sonrise," boomed the announcer.

Jen hugged Sunny with her leg and the mare moved off. Once again they trotted to the far end of the arena, took a running start, and were clear.

Now it was just Jen and Margie.

The wall was raised to 7'8".

The announcer sounded rabid in his excitement. "This

is the current world record folks!"

Sunny cleared it but tipped one of the bricks. Jen heard it give. She looked back over her shoulder after landing. It stayed up.

Margie's gray brought down two bricks.

It was Jenny and Sunny!

The announcer screamed as the arena burst into thunderous applause. Sunny immediately dropped her head in response, just as she'd done at Colton's place. Jen rubbed the mare's mighty neck. "Good girl, Sunny. You're the best."

A familiar shrill voice came over the microphone. *Vanessa DuBois!* "Congratulations, Sunny and Jennifer. You now have to decide if you'd like to attempt to break the world record."

Vanessa DuBois's voice had just the effect she'd hoped. Sunny reared frantically.

As soon as she came down, Jen firmly bent the mare's neck around to prevent another. "Shh, Sunny, it's OK. I am here. She will *not* hurt you anymore."

I need to find her, to let Sunny feel that I've seen her. Jen kept one hand holding the rein as Sunny danced and jumped beneath her. Her other hand tried to shield her eyes from the intense lights.

"Well?" came the voice again. *There! There she is!*

Jen stared straight at the spot where Vanessa DuBois stood. *Now I see her. She's standing in that box!* It was the one place that did not have a spotlight aimed on them. Jen found Vanessa DuBois's eyes. Even from this distance, she saw the twisted smile and cruel expression. Jen urged Sunny closer to the box where Vanessa Dubois stood, hunched over the microphone.

Closer and closer they marched. Sunny's steps grew more confident the closer she got. Jenny kept her gaze soft and relaxed.

"Vanessa DuBois, I forgive you." No one heard, except Jen and Sunny. As soon as the words left her lips, Jen felt overcome by a sense of joy that started at her toes and flooded through the top of her head. She tipped her head back and waited. The crowd grew silent. Sunny quieted as the tension slipped from Jen's body.

Those who wait on the Lord will renew their strength.

They shall mount up like eagles with wings of great length.

"Vanessa DuBois, I forgive you and I choose to love you." Jen's voice sounded tiny and metallic in the arena, but Vanessa DuBois heard. Her angry face crumpled in dismay and she fled the box.

The crowd began chanting, "World record. World record."

Jen grinned toward the judges' box and nodded. The jump crew swarmed from their spots to raise the wall to 7'9".

Jen's eyes scanned the doorway leading to the warm up area. *Daniel! Where's Daniel?* And there he was. Their eyes met. She shrugged the question. He nodded. The crowd gasped as Jen bent Sunny's neck around and slipped the bridle off over her ears. She handed the bridle to Daniel. "This is it, girl. We can do it. We're on eagles' wings." She rubbed Sunny's neck lovingly, then turned and focused on the top of the jump. *Eagles' wings, eagles' wings.*

Sunny broke into a powerful canter. Then . . . at just the right moment . . . they exploded from the ground, Jen's body stretched up over Sunny's neck. It was like being on a rocket going to the moon. They reached the top, hit that heart-stopping place, then descended. It felt like being on a roller coaster at that last big drop before the ride ends. Jen relaxed her body, almost to a slump and Sunny skidded to a stop. They turned to look. The bricks were up!

The arena was dumbstruck for a fraction of a second. Then it erupted in a volley of applause and screaming.

"Eagles' wings, Sunny. That's what you have." Jen leaned forward to hug the mare's neck. Tears of unspeakable joy flowed freely. She sat up and turned in the direction of the warm up door. Mom, Dad, everyone was there, doing the same thing everyone else in the place was doing. Screaming, clapping, and crying.

Thank You, Lord.

Chapter Twenty

They arrived back at Sonrise Farm after 10:00 P.M. Jenny had numerous requests for interviews from television stations and newspapers after the show. She finally enlisted Dad to field questions from the hungry reporters so she could load Sunny and leave.

"We should have gone back to Colton's. That would have lost them," she mused.

"Jen, I am so proud of you *and* Sunny." Dad laughed, squeezing her. "That was the most amazing thing I've *ever* seen!"

She could only grin a delighted grin. "I'm gonna' check Sunny one last time before we head to bed," she said.

She wandered to the barn with a flashlight. Jen heard the rustling sounds before she approached the first corner. She broke into a run. Sunny was just breaking into a sweat. She blinked into the flashlight beam with pain and questions in her dark eyes. *Colic!*

Jen sprinted to the kitchen and with trembling fingers punched the home number for Dr. Dave.

He answered. "Jen!" he exclaimed with delight. "Congratulations!"

"No time, Dr. Dave. Sunny's colicking. We need you now."

"I'm on my way."

There was no need to explain to the folks in the kitchen. They had all heard the conversation. Dan and Kathy sprinted back to the barn with Jen. They began with the medicines they had on hand and walking.

Dr. Davis was there within ten minutes. He checked Sunny's heartbeat and respiration. "Slightly elevated, but not alarming," he smiled reassuringly. He pulled on a long plastic glove. "I'll do a quick palpation and see if she's impacted."

His arm disappeared and Jen rubbed Sunny's neck to reassure her.

"Oh, my!" exclaimed Dr. Davis. "I feel a head!" He pulled his arm out and slipped off the glove. "There's a foal in there, Jen! Sunny's pregnant. Did you know?" He shook his head. "Of course you didn't know. You would never have jumped tonight if you'd known."

Jen's heart leapt, then just as quickly dropped. *A foal!* She stared at Daniel.

Daniel shook his head. "This summer, right after Aunt V evicted Shannon Lockhart, she began telling me to feed Sunny. She quit coming to the barn. I couldn't figure it out. Now I know why. Sunny was pregnant. I don't know who the daddy is, but you can bet he's famous! Aunt V would have chosen the best! Wow!"

"Well," Dr. Davis went on, "this is probably just a mild gas colic. She's got good gut sounds in all four quadrants and her heart rate is normal. I'll stay for a while but I think we're all right." He grinned and patted Sunny gently. "Who would have thought . . ." he shook his head.

That was right after I stopped trying to save Sunny on my own and surrendered her to You, Lord.

"Jen, I have another surprise for you," Dad announced. "We were going to wait until the morning but since we're all out here anyway and not sleepy anymore . . ."

He ushered her toward the car.

"But . . . Sunny," she protested, glancing over her shoulder.

"We're not going far. We'll be right back. Dr. Davis can take care of Sunny for ten minutes."

She climbed into the back seat of the station wagon as Mom and Dad buckled their belts. Dad backed up but instead of heading to the right like he should if he were leaving Sonrise Farm, he turned left.

"Dad! Where are you going? This is the driveway. It ends in about twenty feet at the barn."

"Not any more it doesn't." He grinned as they drove on the new gravel road through some woods, into the glade, and right up to the porch of the little deserted cottage. Only it was no longer a cottage. It had been completely renovated with an addition on each side. A four-stall barn stood where a briar thicket had been. All the brush and trash in the yard was gone.

"We're home!" Dad crowed.

"What do you mean?" Jen could hardly breathe. "Is this ours?"

"Yup, the house and fifteen acres. Mr. O'Riley sold it to us for much less than it is worth. The only condition is that we have to sell it back to him, if we ever sell."

"So is this the 'big project' you've been working on?" she asked, smiling so big she could hardly speak.

"This is it. Want to see your room?"

"Absolutely!"

Jen could only gasp when he threw the door open. On the far wall hung a breath-taking, life-size oil painting of Sunny. The rest of the room looked like hers. Except the bed was new, and the curtains. The desk and all the bookcases were the same. Jen collapsed on the edge of her bed. She could only shake her head.

"Happy Birthday, sweetheart," Dad smiled. "We're home."

"It feels like home." She smiled. "Let's go check on Sunny. Can we sleep here tonight?"

"Of course!" Dad exclaimed. "It's ours."

Sunny looked fine when they returned.

"Just a gas colic," Dr. Dave repeated. "I went ahead and gave her some mineral oil but she's already eating hay. No more jumping on this mare for a while, young lady!" Dr. Dave warned playfully. "Good night. Call me if you need me." He tipped his ten-gallon hat and made his way to the truck.

"Did you see the house?" Kathy asked.

"You knew about this too?" Jen cried.

"I suggested it. Dad thought it was a great idea. He offered it to your folks and *voilà!* We're neighbors."

"Should we move Sunny tonight?" Jen queried.

"No, leave her here," Kathy said. "Daniel's setting up a cot outside her stall. He'll call you if there's a problem. Go home and get some sleep. It's midnight."

"Midnight. Happy Birthday, Jen. It's official." Mom wrapped her up in a big hug.

Dad grinned at both of them. "Some birthday present, Jen," he said. "New house, new car, $250,000! A pretty good day, all said."

🐎 🐎 🐎

Jenny climbed into her new bed in her new room. *Thank You. Thank You, Lord.* She couldn't think of anything else to say.

Please protect Sunny and her unborn foal. I wonder what . . . and she fell asleep.

🐎 🐎 🐎

Jenny Thomas rode the Palomino mare bareback and without a bridle. They raced through the woods into a little glade. Beside the mare ran a spindly Palomino colt.

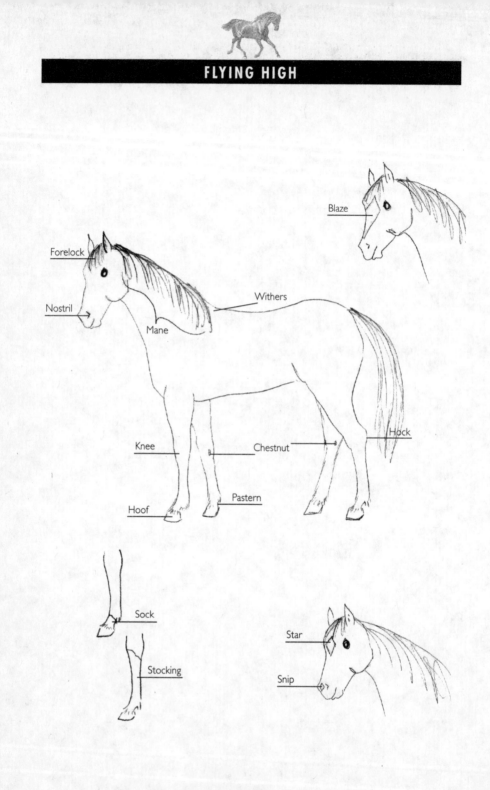

Blaze

Forelock

Nostril

Withers

Mane

Knee

Chestnut

Hock

Hoof

Pastern

Sock

Stocking

Star

Snip

120

Glossary

A

Arabian—An ancient breed of horse from the deserts of Arabia. Arabians are known for their courage, stamina, and beauty.

B

Bay—A color term for a brown horse whose points (bottom part of legs, mane, and tail) are black. Bays may range from a medium brown to almost black (called a seal bay).

Bridle—The leather straps that fit onto the horse's head to keep the bit in place. The bit is the metal part that goes through the horse's mouth. The reins are the connection to the rider.

Broodmare—A female horse whose job is to have foals (baby horses).

Buckskin—A color term for a light brown horse whose points are black. The color of the body may range from a deep gold to sandy. Buckskins may also have a dorsal stripe (a stripe that runs from wither to tail).

C

Canter—One of the four gaits of a horse. Walk, trot, canter, then gallop. Canter is a three-beat gait, usually smooth and easy to ride.

Chestnut—A color term for a plain red horse.

Clydesdale—One of America's most popular draft (working) horses. Clydesdales are huge, (18 hands or more) powerful work horses used for hauling heavy carts or farm machinery. They are usually bay or black in color, with "feathers" (long hair) covering their hooves.

Colic—A term used to describe stomachache in horses. Colic can be deadly serious or simply a bout of gas that passes on its own.

Colt—A young male horse.

Curry comb—A hard rubber brush used to remove deep or caked-on dirt. It should be used vigorously but carefully, because it is hard. It is not used on the lower part of the legs, nor on the face. Once the dirt has been brought to the surface and loosened, it can be brushed away by the softer bristled body brush.

D

Dam—Title for an equine mother. Fury's dam is Sunny.

E

Equine—Scientific name for horses and ponies.

Euthanize—Medical term for destroying an animal. It is usually performed by injecting a deadly substance into the vein. The animal goes to sleep and never wakes. It is painless and fast.

F

Filly—A young female horse.
Foal—A baby horse of either sex.
Founder—A dangerous inflammation inside the hoof. Can be caused by overfeeding or poisoning.

G

Gelding—A castrated (neutered) male horse. Most male horses in the U.S. are geldings. Only horses intended for breeding are maintained as stallions.
Girth—A leather or fabric belt used to keep the saddle on the horse's back. The girth attaches to both sides of the saddle under the belly of the horse.
Grand Prix—The highest level of competitive show jumping
Green—An untrained horse.

H

Hands—A measurement term for horses and ponies. Each hand equals four inches. The horse is measured from the ground to the withers (see parts of the horse diagram). A pony who measures ten hands would be forty inches tall at the withers.
Hoofpick—A hand-sized pick used to remove dirt from the inside of a horse's hoof.
Horse—An equine who measures at least 14:2 hands. That is: fourteen hands and two inches. An animal who

measures 14:2 would be 58 inches at the withers, or 4 feet, 8 inches. At 17 hands Magnum and Sunny stand 5 feet 8 inches at the withers.

I

Impaction—A serious form of colic where something (food or foreign object) blocks the digestive tract.

Inside and Outside reins—A term used to describe the reins as the horse is moving in a circle. Imagine that you are standing in the center of a ring. There is someone riding clockwise around you. The right side of the horse and rider is visible to you. This is the "inside." The left side of the horse and rider is visible from the fence. This is the "outside." If the horse were to change directions, then the left side would be "inside."

M

Mare—An adult female horse.

Morgan—A small strong American breed of horse descended from Justin Morgan's famous little bay stallion of the late 1700s.

Mucking Out—Cleaning a stall.

N

Nicker—A low chuckling sound horses make when they see someone or something they love.

P

Paddock—A small enclosure, usually less than an acre in size.

Palomino—A color breed whose coat is the color of a newly minted gold coin. The mane and tail should be platinum.

Platinum—A precious metal that is almost white in color.

Post—The action of rising and sitting in the saddle while your mount is trotting. The reason for posting during the trot is to reduce the jarring that occurs.

R

Ratcatcher—A shirt worn when showing. It has a high collar around the neck and is secured with a bow.

Registered—Each individual breed of horse and pony has a registry, or a list of its members. The registered horses can then trace their ancestry. The Jockey Club of America also requires all racing Thoroughbreds to be tattooed on the inside of the upper lip. This stands as permanent proof of a horse's identity. Sunny, being tattooed, is a registered Thoroughbred. All Jenny needs to do to find Sunny's bloodlines is call the Jockey Club and tell them the number on Sunny's lip. They will be able to look up Sunny's bloodlines.

Rig—Truck and trailer together

S

Sire—Title for an equine father. We don't know who Fury's sire is.

Snaffle—A mild shankless bit that is broken in the middle. The fatter the snaffle, the milder its action.

Stallion—An ungelded (unneutered) adult male horse. Usually difficult to handle.

Stocking—A color term used to describe a leg that is white up to the knee (in front) or the hock (in back). See parts of the horse diagram.

T

Tack—The name given to the collection of stuff that goes on a horse. Saddle, bridle, girth, etc. May also be used as a verb, to mean putting all the stuff onto the horse.

Thoroughbred—A breed of horse known for its long graceful limbs and athletic ability. Thoroughbred horses are used in horse racing.

U

Untack—The act of removing the saddle and bridle from a horse.

W

Weanling—Colts and fillies who are between six and twelve months old. Most horses are removed from their mothers (weaned) at six months. At twelve months of age they are referred to as yearlings.

Welsh Pony—A lovely hardy breed of pony that originated in Wales (a small country next to England).

Whicker—Similar to nicker.

If you love horses . . .
Come to Sonrise Farm!

What do rowdy racoons, missing reindeer, and mutant killer mega-wasps have in common?

They're all GREAT stories in *The Midnight Raccoon Alarm*, the newest **Great Stories for Kids** book by Jerry Thomas.

If you like stories full of adventure, surprise, mystery, and fun, you'll love *The Midnight Raccoon Alarm*. Besides stories about camping, purple cows, a school play, and other stuff, you'll get to see how other kids handled some of the things you have to deal with. Things like being afraid, making good decisions, and dealing with bad language.

The Midnight Raccoon Alarm is book 3 in Jerry D. Thomas's **Great Stories for Kids** series, and there are four more that are just as exciting! Collect them all and enjoy 133 GREAT stories and pictures that will make you jump back, laugh out loud, and keep you guessing what will happen next!